# The Bargain

## Vargas Cartel Series, Book 1

Lisa Cardiff

The Bargain

Limitless Publishing, LLC
Kailua, HI 96734
www.limitlesspublishing.com

Formatting: Limitless Publishing

ISBN-13: 978-1-68058-077-8
ISBN-10: 1-68058-077-9

# Prologue

Murmurs. Whispers. Papers shuffled. A door opened.

I tried to move, but I couldn't.

I opened my eyes, but everything was black.

I wanted to scream, but my mouth was full.

I jerked my body forward, but fire roared through my shoulders. Holy shit...I was tied to a chair. Ropes bit into my wrists and my ankles, burning my skin with every quiver and twist of my extremities.

I didn't have a fucking clue where I was. I didn't recall anything. My mind spun in relentless circles searching for a memory, a clue, anything to explain where I was or what happened to me. Jumbled thoughts whipped through my brain in rapid-fire succession.

Spring Break.

Mexico.

Dancing in a nightclub.

A Prairie Fire.

An Irish Car Bomb.

A Red Headed Slut.

A Buttery Nipple.

So many others I couldn't name them all.

One song blurring into the next.

Dancing on the bar.

And *him*.

Someone ripped the hood from my head, taking a few strands of hair with it. Bright light seared my eyeballs. I squeezed them closed, willing them to adjust to the light. When I opened them again, a bone-jarring jolt of recognition raced through me. I saw *him*...the guy from the bar. Ryker. Dark, almost black hair, icy gray eyes, straight nose and angular features, enhanced by the careless, dark stubble on his face. What the hell?

He snatched my hair, twisting it around his hand until my scalp stung. One calloused finger trailed down the side of my face almost reverently. I twisted my head to the side, but he yanked me back.

He chuckled, his too lush lips forming a twisted smile. "What's wrong? You liked my touch last night."

I screamed, but the dusty rag in my mouth muffled my voice. I tried to spit it out, but my mouth was too dry. Tears erupted from behind my eyes, and water streamed down my face.

What did he want? Was he going to kill me? Did he plan to rape me?

Just like that my stomach revolted. He won't rape me. He already had me. Images of my dress around my waist, his pants unzipped, and my body pressed against a dirty stucco wall as he moved inside of me flickered through my mind. I gagged and inhaled at the same time. My lungs burned. My heart jackhammered against my breastbone. My ears howled. Black dots clouded my vision. My head rolled forward.

"Calm the fuck down. You're going to faint." He ripped the rag from my mouth, and I opened my mouth, preparing to scream, but he moved faster. His hand had slammed over my mouth before I had the opportunity to summon a single syllable.

"If you scream, I'll shove that rag back into your mouth so hard you'll lose your front teeth."

My head bobbed up and down like a bobble head doll.

Slowly, his hand lifted from my mouth, and my mind cleared. I remembered who I am and what that meant. "You'll regret this. Do you know who I am?"

His lips curved into a smile, not the carefree, sexy smile he used on me at the bar. It made me feel dirty. I wanted to scour my skin for hours. "You're Hattie Covington."

I didn't remember sharing my full name last night. I never shared it. I preferred to be anonymous. My name carried too much baggage, especially in my circle of friends, but Ryker wasn't part of my circle and he certainly wasn't my friend. Far from it. He was a random guy from a random bar. "And do you know what that means?" I hissed through clenched teeth. I wanted to sound strong and brave, but my voice cracked on the last word, shredding the illusion.

He tipped up my chin, brushing his finger across my lower lip. I flinched, but he didn't notice, or if he did, he didn't care…probably the latter.

"Ah, that's cute. Do you and your friends really say that?" he mocked with far too much amusement.

"My dad is the Attorney General of the United States," I yelled.

"And that's exactly why you're here."

# Chapter One

*Three weeks ago...*

"What time do you want me to pick you up tonight?" Evan asked as we strolled out of our last class of the day. Evan and I started dating in college. We were both political science majors and both of our dads were career politicians. We moved in similar circles, our parents knew each other, one thing led to another, and we started dating. We even applied to the same graduate schools. Everyone expected us to get married sooner rather than later, and we probably would—Evan had been dropping hints about asking me to marry him for the last couple months.

Admittedly, we didn't have an earth shattering, yell from the rooftops love affair, but we were comfortable in each other's lives; we had similar goals, and I loved him. Evan wanted to follow his father into politics, and I wanted to find a job working in foreign policy. I dreamed of working in the State Department, and with my connections and my master's degree, I could make it happen. I had already secured an internship when I graduated this spring at the American Foreign Policy Council.

"Shit," I said under my breath. Tonight was the fundraiser for his dad. Evan's dad was a second, soon-to-be third term Senator of Nevada. Before entering politics, Evan's dad owned a casino, so he has connections to people with deep pockets. The D.C. fundraiser probably wasn't necessary, but in politics a well-funded campaign almost always translated into a winning campaign.

Evan stopped walking. "Don't tell me you forgot, because we both know you never forget anything."

"Maybe I did forget. There's a first time for everything," I lied, looking down at my simple black wedges. Of course I didn't forget. I methodically planned every hour of every day right down to the most mundane detail, like when I planned to exercise, study, and eat. I reviewed my schedule for the next day every night before I went to bed. Nothing was a surprise.

I realized planning my life with such precision likely meant I had some sort of obsessive disorder, but it gave me control over my life, something I didn't have much of as a kid. Growing up, my mom selected my clothes, my hairstyle, my friends, and my enemies. She arranged my play dates and planned my meals and snacks so that I never exceeded my allotted caloric intake.

I lived my life as her puppet until the day I left for college. Now I ruled my life with iron control and absolute clockwork precision, so she didn't have the chance to slide back into my life and make decisions for me.

Wrapping his hands around my upper arms, he turned my body to face him. His eyes narrowed and his mouth pressed into a thin line. "Really, Hattie? Do you expect me to believe that you forgot? Let me see your phone."

I lifted my head, meeting the irritated stare of his chocolate brown eyes.

"I put it in my phone, but Eric called in sick with a family emergency, and I agreed to cover his office hours." Eric was in the same graduate program as Evan and me. His mom had cancer, and it had been a rough year for him. I covered his office hours at least once a week to give him more time to help her.

"Eric always has a family emergency," Evan snapped, folding his arms across his chest.

"I know, but his mom has a chemo treatment today. I had to help him. She can't go by herself." It wasn't too late to call him and cancel. He'd find someone else or he could reschedule his hours, but I didn't want to add to Eric's stress. He had all he needed and more.

"Don't be mad." I lifted onto my toes and brushed a kiss over his lips. I didn't have to look at his face to know he was pissed. Attending a fundraiser for Evan's dad was a big deal, but I had been dreading it for the last month. My parents would be there, and that meant my mom wouldn't hold back when the time came to judge my clothing choices, my hair, and my behavior. Like always, she'd go on a tirade about Evan and me having a big future in politics and I needed to dress and look the part. A chill raced through me at the thought of enduring another confrontation with her. I wished she'd back off and leave me alone for once.

At least Evan asked me to move in with him when we started graduate school, and I escaped the prison of living at home. I could've rented my own place after college, but I didn't like living alone. My parents didn't provide much companionship, but being alone would have been infinitely worse.

"I'm not mad." He brushed his thumb over my lip. "But I have to admit the events are more tolerable when I have you on my arm."

"Oh please." I rolled my eyes. "You barely talk to me at those events. I could give you a cardboard cutout of myself, and it'd be just as effective."

He chuckled, flashing his bright white smile, and one of his hands slipped to my lower back. "No. I'd notice when I ended up with a bunch of paper cuts."

I grinned at him. "Jerk," I joked.

"What time do office hours end?"

"It's only two hours, so I'll be done by nine."

He slid my hair behind my ear. "Don't wait up for me. I'll be home late. I'm meeting the guys at that bar on K Street after I've put in enough face time to satisfy my dad. There's a good band playing there tonight."

My brows scrunched together. "I don't remember you mentioning that before." I didn't like Evan's friends. For the most part, they were a bunch of entitled assholes with a cruel sense of humor.

"I'm sure I mentioned it." He kneaded the back of his neck, his face utterly blank.

"What's wrong?" Massaging the back of his neck usually meant something was amiss or he was hiding information. He didn't realize he did it. I should've told him. Obvious tells weren't beneficial in politics, but I liked being able to read him.

His eyes flickered to the side and then a huge smile flashed across his face. "Nothing. I'll miss you tonight." He threaded his fingers through mine and guided me toward his car. "Are you ready to go home?" He never wanted to rush back to our apartment after class. Normally, he had a million and one things to do.

"I could meet you at the bar. I'll be done by nine, and if no one shows, I can leave early." I squeezed his hand, pulling him closer to me as we walked to the parking lot. "We can have a few drinks and be in bed by ten-thirty." I flashed him a naughty grin letting him know exactly what I meant. Over the last month, we'd been so busy our sex life had suffered. Not that we were ever too crazy, but now we lived like roommates instead a young couple in love. That didn't bode well for the future, but I tried to push the thought out of my mind and mentally recite all the reasons we were perfect for each other.

"You don't have to come. I understand." He stopped next to his car and I tried to catch his eyes, but they roamed everywhere except to me. "I know you don't like my friends."

"What?" A completely fake laugh slipped from my lips. "I never said that."

"You didn't have to. It's obvious."

I bit on the side of my lower lip. "I'm that transparent, huh?"

He tapped my nose. "Don't be upset. I think it's cute you can't hide your emotions…especially when it comes to me." He lowered his voice. "I like that you're mine, and you've only been with me." By all accounts, Evan hadn't been an angel before he met me, but it never bothered me. Once we met, we clicked, and that's all that counted anyway. His reputation as a womanizer quickly disappeared, and for the most part, he'd never given me a reason to doubt him.

My cheeks heated and I ducked my head. "You're embarrassing me," I whined even as I smiled at him.

"I'm not trying to." He pressed a kiss on my forehead, and then he opened the passenger door of his car for me.

"If I can leave Eric's office hours early, I'll meet you at the bar," I reaffirmed. I did want to spend time with him. I owed it to him for missing the fundraiser.

# Chapter Two

"I can't believe you dragged me here. This place smells like stale beer and vomit," Vera said as we pushed our way through the crowd of people.

The band had started playing about a half an hour ago, and I was late, but I still wanted to meet Evan, so I came anyway. I'd texted him, but he didn't respond.

After nearly fifteen minutes of searching, I spotted a couple of Evan's friends sitting at a table near the stage. Evan wasn't at the table, but they probably knew where to find him.

"Hey," I said as I stood near the edge of the table.

"Hi," Darren and Matt replied, hardly looking in my direction. My dislike was mutual. At first, I tried to be friendly, but they were a bad influence on Evan. He always drank too much and did stupid shit when they were around.

I tipped my head toward Vera. "Do you guys remember Vera?"

They nodded as though it were too much effort

to say anything. Vera hated them even more than I did. Unlike me though, she didn't hold back.

"I'm going to get us a drink. What do you want?" Vera asked.

"A beer."

"That narrows it down."

I rolled my eyes. "Just order two of whatever you want."

She chuckled as she walked away. "I have the perfect drink."

I sat at one of the two empty seats at the table. "Have you seen Evan?"

Darren smirked. "I think he went to the bathroom."

Matt elbowed him and shook his head, his eyes narrowed.

"What?" Darren said. "She asked. I answered."

"Right," Matt said, drawing out the word. "You're totally innocent."

My eyes bounced between them. Obviously, I missed some important information. "I'll be back."

I pressed through the people crowding the dance floor, heading toward the bathrooms located at the end of the hall. Evan and I came to this bar more than a few times to listen to the live music, so I knew where to find the bathroom.

I turned the corner near the edge of the dance floor intending to wait for Evan. Every muscle in my body turned to cement when I saw him. My stomach knotted, and my heart spiraled to a painful stop. I rubbed my eyes, unwilling to believe what I saw at the end of the hallway.

Evan stood at the end of the hall, his body

smashed against some blonde-haired woman in a short blue dress, her arms locked around his neck. With his tongue halfway down her throat and one of his hands under her skirt, his body moved against hers in a rhythm that made my dinner lurch in my stomach.

The live music reverberated harshly through my ears. Anger and betrayal pumped like acid through my veins. Hot tears seared the corners of my eyes and my hands fisted the fabric of my dress. I tried to blink away the evidence of my shattering heart and be strong, but the tears kept coming, refusing to leave my dignity intact.

Part of me wanted to bolt for the door and drink enough alcohol to burn the image from my eyes, but the rest of me wanted to rip every last strand of Evan's perfectly gelled hair from his head.

"Evan," I yelled, but his name clotted in my throat.

He lifted his head, and his dark eyes locked with mine.

"Hattie, baby," he said pushing away from the woman. "I'm sorry." He held out his hand to me— the same one that had been up that woman's dress five seconds earlier—and I felt something break inside me beyond recognition. My heart? Trust? I didn't know.

I backpedaled a few steps, shaking my head from side to side, my short hair whipping my cheeks. "Don't touch me." A dozen fragmented thoughts collided in my brain, but my mouth floundered. The ability to focus escaped me. Was this the first time he'd cheated? Or did it happen so often that he wasn't worried about me catching him in the act? Was he dating this woman too? Were there others? Did his friends know?

"Evan," the blonde woman said as her bubblegum fingernails dug into the skin on his forearm. "What's going on?"

He snatched his arm out of her grasp, keeping his glued to mine. "Lena, you need to leave. You were a mistake. It's over."

Her heavily made-up blue eyes widened for a minute and then she marched past him, her shoulder knocking into mine. "Go to hell. You said you weren't dating her anymore," she yelled, her finger waving in my direction. "Don't call me again. I'm done with your games."

With those few words, she confirmed I hadn't interrupted a one-time hookup. I put a hand on my stomach willing the contents to stay put.

"It's not as bad as it looks." Evan took a tentative step toward me.

"You're right."

Relief caused his face to sag, and he blew out a long exaggerated breath. "Let me—"

He actually thought I'd fall for his dumb excuses. "It's worse," I interrupted. "How many times?"

His eyebrows scrunched together, marring the smooth skin between his dark eyes. "What are you talking about?"

"How many times have you cheated?"

"Baby, what happened tonight will never happen again. We're good together. Don't throw it away over a little misstep."

"A misstep? It won't happen again." I echoed his words as the tears blurred my vision until I felt like I was looking through a prism into an alternate reality. "What does that mean? You're insane if you think I'll believe anything that falls out of your mouth right now."

He slammed his hand on the wall, with a dark scowl. "I had too much to drink. She pulled me onto the dance floor and before I knew it, one thing—"

I held up my hand and willed it not to shake. "Don't try to pull that shit with me. I don't care if you drank a fifth of vodka. It doesn't give you a license to cheat, much less shove your hand up some slut's skirt." My voice shattered on the last word. I can't believe four years of dating Evan boiled down to this moment in a stupid bar. It felt like an out of body experience where I floated above my body watching the train wreck unfold second by second.

"Fuck," he yelled, his eyebrows slanting downward. For a split second, I fantasized about clawing his eyes out. "What can I do to make this better? I can't lose you. I love you."

"Jesus. I'm not stupid. Don't treat me like I am." I rubbed the back of my hand over my eyes. I'm sure I had rings of mascara dripping down my face. I needed to get control of myself. I didn't like being the crazy girl, screaming at my boyfriend in public while everyone stared in sick fascination, and I definitely sensed eyes on us—judging me, judging Evan, watching the destruction of my relationship. "I can't talk to you right now, not here, and not tonight." I paused, and a shudder rolled through me.

"Don't wait up for me tonight. I'm not going home."

"No. Don't do that." He reached for me again, but I took a giant step back. The thought of him touching me made me sick. "I'll sleep on the couch."

"No," I shook my head, whipping it from side to side. "I can't be around you. I can't be anywhere near you. Not tonight. Not tomorrow." I turned and ran before he stopped me. My body ricocheted off the elbows, knees, and shoulders of faceless people as I threaded through the crowd. I didn't stop to apologize. I needed to flee before the weight of Evan's betrayal swallowed me whole.

# Chapter Three

"Evan is downstairs again," my mom said standing in the doorway of my childhood bedroom, the room I'd been using since I walked away from Evan. Over two weeks had slipped by, and I still hadn't emailed, texted, or talked to Evan, and I didn't have any intention of changing course now. Our relationship was over. I'd have to talk to him eventually, and I needed to get my things from his place, but I didn't want to do it yet.

"Tell him to go away," I responded without looking up from my computer. I buried myself in research for my graduate advisor, trying to ignore Evan and what happened.

"Look at me," she barked.

I hid my smile. She hated being ignored. I lifted my head and painted a fake smile on my face. "Yes?"

Elegant, ageless, and as cold on the inside as on the outside, my mom braced one expertly manicured hand on her hip. Her blood red fingertips contrasted with her stiff navy dress. "I'm growing tired of this childish game you're playing with Evan. You need to talk to him. He's sorry. That's all that matters. Don't throw away everything we've worked for. Evan is your future."

I slammed my laptop closed and stood up. "No, mom. He's not my future. I don't want to be with him now or ever."

"Well, you need to alter your opinion because it's a done deal. You're going to marry Evan. That's what everyone expects, and that's what you're going to do." With one graceful flick of her hand, she pushed her subtly highlighted blonde hair away from her face.

"If you like Evan so much, then you marry him, because I don't intend to welcome him back into my life anytime in the next decade."

"Grow up, Hattie. You've made commitments and the Covington's never go back on their word. You're going to his family's house in the Virgin Islands in a week. It's time to move on. You've made your point. Gather your things and go home with Evan."

"Actually, I'm not going to the Virgin Islands. I exchanged my ticket last night." I folded my arms across my chest and smiled.

"Exchanged it for what?" My mom's surprise was evident in her eyes and the rigidness of her spine. If not for her regular Botox injections, her eyebrows would have been hidden beneath the elegant sweep of her light brown hair.

"I'm going to Mexico with Vera."

"Vera." My best friend's name rolled off her tongue like a curse. She never liked Vera. She thought Vera was too expressive and uncouth…whatever that meant. Personally, I attributed her dislike to the fact that Vera's dad dropped out of politics five years ago, and he didn't even pretend he cared about his former colleagues or former profession, except my dad. They still played poker once a month in what Vera's dad deemed a 'politics free zone.'

"Yes." I raised one eyebrow. "Is there something wrong with that? Dad was fine with it." I lied. I didn't ask him, but he wouldn't care. He liked Evan, but he wouldn't interfere. Besides, at my age, I didn't need parental permission, and I was sick of my mom pretending otherwise. I really needed to find a place to live, because hanging out in my childhood bedroom sucked.

My mom tapped her fingernails on the doorjamb without saying a word, but it didn't mean my mom wasn't thinking, calculating, and manipulating facts in her mind. I think her ruthlessness exceeded my dad's, and that said a lot. "Fine," she said. "But you will give Evan the respect he deserves and tell him about your plans face to face."

My eyes narrowed and I wanted to refuse, but I didn't. I had to face him at some point, and now would work as well as any other day. "Send him up."

"He's in the living room."

*No way.* I rolled my eyes. My mom wanted to eavesdrop and do damage control if necessary. I didn't want her to listen and report every detail to my dad. Over the last two weeks, she'd done everything she could think of to force me to

Lisa Cardiff

reconcile with Evan, except hold a gun to my head. "So." I shrugged. "I'm sure his legs work."

She walked away without saying another word.

Five minutes later, Evan walked into my room, his hands buried in the front pockets of his khaki chinos, his face clean shaven, his white dress shirt expertly starched, all tied together with a brown belt and loafers. He might as well have been a mannequin with his utter lack of uniqueness. Why hadn't I noticed that before?

"Hi," he said softly as he sat next to me on the edge of the bed.

"Hi." I tucked my legs beneath my black maxi dress, purposely leaving my toes exposed. I painted my toenails metallic blue yesterday in silent rebellion against Evan. I knew he would hate it, and judging from the direction of his gaze, he had noticed.

Last Easter, I painted them the light blue to match my light blue linen suit. I thought they added a fun flare to my boring suit. Evan didn't concur. He berated me the entire drive home from the brunch at his parents' country club. Apparently, he thought they looked tacky and unprofessional. At the time, I didn't really care. It was nail polish, not a tattoo. I could switch it out easily enough, but now his comment symbolized something bigger—his gamble to control and groom me for a role I no longer wanted. His wife.

"Thanks for seeing me."

I nodded, unwilling to be the first person to delve into the details of what happened or what it meant for our future. Anger and resentment ricocheted around the room.

"I miss you. When are you coming home?" he inquired, breaking the silence and diving into the heart of our conflict.

"I'm not."

"Why not?"

I snorted. "Seriously, Evan. I caught you with your hand up some woman's dress. Do I need to have another reason, because that one seems pretty good to me?"

Evan rubbed the back of his neck. "How can I change your mind? How can I make this better?"

I blew out an exaggerated breath. "Evan, I don't think you can. I can't pretend I didn't see you with that woman. When I look at you, it's all I see. I don't know if what happened was a one-time thing, or if it was one of many—"

"Hattie," he interrupted, claiming my hands, his thumbs coasting along the inside of my wrists. "I promise it won't happen again. I'm not going to lie. I haven't been perfect for the last four years, but losing you over a thoughtless decision reformed me for good. You have my word. I won't cheat ever again. You're my future."

I seesawed between overwhelming sadness and rage. I swallowed hard, trying to hold back the flood of emotions, but my throat was too dry and constricted to finish the motion. "Wow. I don't know what to say," I whispered, the rawness in my voice unmistakable. I jerked my hands out of his grasp. I felt as though I was dying inch by slow inch. The last four years had been a lie, and I'd been blind and dumb to reality. Evan hadn't changed. He wouldn't change. Ever.

"I know it's not what you wanted to hear, but I'm not going to lie and have to revisit this issue again. I want to put everything on the table so we can put it behind us. This way, we'll have a clean slate again without any secrets hovering over us. It wasn't as bad as you're thinking. When we first started dating, occasionally I hooked up with another woman, but that stopped after two or three months when I realized I only wanted you. I never touched anyone else until two weeks ago. I went to a bar and Lena sat next to me."

I held my hands over my ears. "I don't want to know the details. Jesus, I get the point."

"No." He yanked my hands away from my face. "Let me finish. We danced. We kissed. After that, we went to dinner a couple times while you were at work. Then, she showed up at the bar the night you…" Evan looked away and rubbed the side of his face. "Found us. I didn't invite her. We never had sex…not one time."

I tipped my head toward the ceiling, the emptiness in my heart expanding to epic proportions with each passing word. "I appreciate your honesty, but I'm not ready to forgive you." No, that wasn't the truth. I'd never be able to have a trusting relationship with him again. Just thinking about how many times I crawled into bed next to him when he'd been with someone else sent a shard of pain through my foolish heart until it was nothing but a splintered mess in my chest.

"Not seeing you is tearing me apart." He pinched the bridge of his nose. "These past two weeks, I've been thinking about why I cheated."

I lifted my eyebrows. "And what'd you come up with?" I prompted.

"I missed us. We used to spend all our time together, and lately you've been busy—"

"Don't blame this on me."

He shook his head. "I'm not, but I want more of you than you've been giving me. I want things to be like they were before graduate school."

"I don't know, Evan. Everything fluctuates over time. Between classes, work, fundraisers for your dad, and graduation, neither of us has much left to give. This break is probably a good thing."

"Don't give up on us. When it's just the two of us next week, we can get past this...find a compromise."

My eyes darted to the side. "Evan, I'm not going with you. I already canceled my flight."

"What?" He stood up, two spots of color staining his cheekbones, his eyes dark with anger.

"I'm going to Playa del Carmen with Vera."

"Fuck, Hattie." He tugged at the roots of his sandy brown hair, causing gelled strands of hair to stick up in frazzled clumps. "You're really going to throw us away over a few mistakes." He pointed a finger at me. "You're not perfect either, but I'm willing to overlook your faults. Can't you do the same for me?"

And there was the arrogant Evan I knew. "I may have worked too late on occasion, and I know I'm not as spontaneous as you'd like, but I never cheated. Not once." I cradled my body with my arms. "I never even considered it."

"No, you're right. I'm sorry," he said almost soundlessly, dropping his head to his chest. "So where does this leave us?"

I stood up and walked to my door. He needed to leave. "There isn't an us. At least, not now."

"I'm not giving up. I love you."

He wrapped his arms around me and brushed his lips across my forehead. I stood frozen in his arms, not reciprocating, but not moving. I missed him. I missed my perfectly arranged life, but I needed to let it go.

"I can't promise you anything," I whispered into crook of his neck.

"I know." He released me and took a few steps back. "I have to meet my dad in twenty minutes, but this isn't over. We'll talk after Spring Break."

"Bye, Evan," I said, not acknowledging his words. Evan didn't want to give up on me, but I wouldn't give in either. I couldn't, not if I wanted to regain control over my life, and I did…more than anything.

# Chapter Four

"You're wearing this." Vera, my best and only true friend, tossed a black, silky dress, resembling lingerie at my face. Other than Vera, my friends had taken Evan's side. They accused me of overreacting. Fuck them. I didn't need them.

"No, thanks." I tossed the dress on the hotel bed next to me. "I'm not going out tonight."

She cocked one leg to the side and balanced one hand on her hip. "Why not? We're in Mexico. We can't sit in our hotel room like two losers."

"You can go without me. I don't mind." I didn't mind. In fact, I preferred it. That way, I'd have more time to sulk without worrying about Vera's feelings. I needed to pull my head out of my ass and stop being a bad friend, and I would, but not tonight.

"That's dumb. I'm not going without you."

"Just go. I'm sunburned. I'll be miserable." I thumbed through the gossip magazine I picked up in the airport, pretending to be totally absorbed in the story of the latest starlet gone crazy. In truth, my

25

misery demanded all of my attention. I didn't have room in my life for other people's problems and Vera clearly noticed. When Vera convinced me to go on this vacation with her, enjoying myself seemed like a foregone conclusion. Now, it felt like another obstacle, preventing me from putting shattered pieces of my life back into order.

Vera flipped her vibrant red hair over her shoulder. "Nope. That excuse won't work. You didn't leave the beach cabana once today, and you have olive skin."

I tilted my head to the side. "I swam laps in the morning." At home, I alternated between swimming and running on a daily basis. Exercise kept my life organized, structured…just the way I liked it. I didn't like to deviate from my routine, and the last three weeks had been a huge deviation. I ran in a different park. I swam at a different gym. I slept in a different bed. I left my favorite coffee mug at my old apartment with Evan.

"For twenty minutes at sunrise. That hardly counts. Try again."

"My stomach hurts?" I said it as a question. Both of us knew there wasn't a thing wrong with me except a wounded ego. I didn't want Evan back, but it sickened me that I wasted so much time with him. I completely misread him until he shoved his true self in my face in the form of a buxom blonde. Even worse, my mom refused to let the idea of a happily ever after for Evan and me die.

She rolled her eyes. "You're going out with me tonight. I won't take no for an answer. We're on a mission."

"Oh really?" I dropped the magazine in my lap and folded my arms across my chest. "Please share."

Vera chewed on her lower lip for a second before answering. "We're going to find the hottest guy in the bar and you're going to bring him back here and fuck Evan out of your life for good."

My eyebrows scaled my forehead, disappearing under my blunt cut bangs. "Sorry…that's not going to happen. I'm not going to stop being me because Evan is a complete and total manwhore." Evan was my first and only boyfriend. Except for a kiss, I'd given him my first everything. I wasn't a paragon of virtue who had saved myself for the right guy. On the contrary, I was the quintessential late bloomer. At five feet ten, I towered over most guys in high school, and I didn't have a curve or anything resembling a chest until I turned eighteen.

My lack of feminine attributes weren't relevant, because my mom had forbidden me from dating until my senior year. By then I had focused all my attention on doing the right activities to secure admission to the right college to get as far away from my mom as possible. I dated in college a little, but nothing serious until I met Evan at the end of my sophomore year. We were political science majors, and we had friends in common. From the minute we met, we were inseparable, and then we went to the same graduate school.

"We'll see." Vera moved to the edge of the bed. She lifted the dress I had crumbled into a ball and held it out in front of her. "This will look sexy on you."

"It won't fit me. I'm five inches taller than you, and you have considerably more going on in the chest than me." Vera's body resembled a 1950's pinup girl. Sexiness oozed from her pores like perfume, and today wasn't any exception. She looked amazing in her short emerald green halter dress.

I realized a long time ago I couldn't pull off the sexy thing, so I went for sophistication. I had dark brown hair, cut in a blunt bob with long bangs, brown eyes on a bad day, and hazel on a good day.

"Your legs will look amazing in this. You spend all your free time running and swimming. You should show off your hard work."

"Oh please," I said rolling my eyes. "I'll look like the lanky girl who forgot to change out of her pajamas."

"Put it on. You'll see. "

I groaned and held out my hand. "Fine. Give it to me. I don't care if my ass hangs out the bottom of the dress. Nobody will look at me anyway, especially when you're standing next to me."

"That's not true. I'd kill to have your long legs, and it's not always a good thing to have huge breasts. Do you realize how many guys start a conversation with my chest instead of me?"

"Whatever. At least guys talk to you."

"Don't be such a buzz kill. You've been wrapped up in Evan for too long. Guys would talk to you if you showed any interest."

I lifted the dress up in front of me, eyeing it skeptically. "And this dress is your idea of me showing interest."

"It's a start." She turned and walked toward the bathroom. "You have thirty minutes to get ready."

"I don't need half that long." I planned to slip the dress on, put on some clear lip gloss and a pair of sandals. I needed all of ten minutes to complete the look.

"Yes, you do, because I'm helping you get dressed. You know what that means?" Vera announced as she glanced over her shoulder, a sly smile on her berry colored lips.

"No, but I'm sure you'll share," I said flatly.

"We're going big, which means shaving, exfoliating, and full war paint."

"*Fan-fucking-tastic*, so guys will be soliciting me for a blowjob in the alley."

Vera furrowed her eyebrows. "Don't insult me. You'll look perfect. Beautiful."

I smiled faintly. "I know. I'm just giving you a hard time for making me go."

"You won't regret it. I promise. This is going to be one of the most memorable nights of our lives."

# Chapter Five

An hour later, we walked into a bar filled with more people than was safe or sanitary. Music vibrated from the speakers set in the thatched roof, causing it to shake. Red, blue, and purple lights flashed in time with the music. A woman in a black halter-top and black booty shorts carried a tray of tequila shots.

It was so far out of my realm of experience, I took a step backward from culture shock. Boring political fundraisers and quiet dinners with Evan were more my speed, or at least since I met Evan. Sure, I went to bars too, but this bar was crazier than the places I frequented at home.

"Go with it," Vera said.

"Do you see anyone?" The rest of our friends left the hotel a half hour earlier. Vera fussed over my hair, makeup, and shoe selection for nearly an hour, but when she finished my mouth fell open. I never wore much makeup, but Vera did this smoky-eyed, red lipstick thing, and I went from dully sophisticated to mysteriously sexy.

The Bargain

Standing on her tiptoes, she scanned the crowd. "No, but we need a drink. We'll run into them at some point." She linked her arm through mine and pulled me through the masses of hot sweaty bodies, grinding against each other toward the bar.

A few well-placed elbows here and there and I stood smashed between two people at the bar. "Tequila shot?" I asked Vera, glancing over my shoulder. I might as well start with the strong stuff. With any luck, it'd keep my negative thoughts at bay…or amplify them so I morphed into a messy, tear-stained drunk.

"Nope." She held up a bar menu she snagged off one of the tables, waving it in front of my face. "We are going to have every shot on this list."

I scanned the list and raised one eyebrow. "I don't have any interest in seeing the inside of a Mexican hospital tonight or ever."

She shoved my shoulder playfully, and I teetered sideways on my ridiculously high heels right into the person next to me. He didn't notice.

"Not all of them. I was just messing with you. Let's start with a…" She ran her finger down the menu with her eyes closed. Her eyes popped open, and her finger stopped.

I leaned over and squinted to bring the words into focus when the strobe light flashed. "A Prairie Fire?"

Vera scrunched up her nose and groaned. "I guess the gods have spoken."

"Do you realize what's in that shot?"

"Yeah, but we're letting fate take over tonight, so a Prairie Fire it is."

31

Lisa Cardiff

I shook my head. "I have a feeling I'm going to regret going out tonight."

"Regrets mean you had fun. Stop being so whiny."

Three shots later and we had imbibed enough liquid courage to climb on top of the bar and dance with a few random girls. I twirled, twisted, and rocked my hips back and forth. Guys gathered around the bar, cheering us on and touching me way more than I liked, but I decided to go with it. This was my last Spring Break before I graduated. I would go with the flow, even if it killed me.

"I have to use the bathroom. I'll be back in a few minutes," I yelled next to Vera's ear, two body shots and more than an hour later. I didn't need to go. My arches were crying for relief from my four-inch heels, and I needed to sit down. Unfortunately, Vera looked as though she didn't have any intention of stopping anytime soon, which meant I was on my own for a while.

"Wait." Her hand looped around my forearm. "Look over there." She tipped her head toward the far end of the bar.

My eyes drifted over the faces of the people. "Can you be more specific? What am I looking at?"

"Are you really that clueless?" She elbowed me in the ribs. "Mr. Dark and Sexy sitting at the end of the bar. He hasn't taken his eyes off you for the last ten minutes." She lowered her voice even though the music was loud enough to be heard three blocks away. "I think we may have found the man to wipe away any lingering messy feelings you have for Evan."

"I told you I'm not hooking up with a random guy."

"When you see him, you'll change your mind."

With my heart hammering against my ribcage, I pushed my hair behind ear, and I turned my head sideways again, trying to be inconspicuous. *Holy hell.* The most insanely good-looking man I'd ever seen sat not more than twenty feet away. How did I miss him? One glance and thoughts of twisted sheets and a hot, sweaty night flashed through my mind.

When my eyes connected with his, all the air rushed out of my lungs, my nipples tightened, and my hands shook. "Wow," I whispered, mostly to myself as I quickly lowered my eyes.

Vera grinned like a maniac. "My thoughts exactly." She nudged my back. "Go get him."

"Maybe I need another shot first. We haven't sampled the Buttery Nipple." Everything about the way he watched me said he wanted to talk to me, and a whole lot more. Rather than giving me confidence, the knowledge sent a ripple of uncertainty through my alcohol-filled stomach. I didn't know the first thing about flirting or random hookups, and the way he looked at me made me nervous in a way I couldn't remember feeling since starring in my high school play at the age of sixteen.

Vera elbowed me in the side. "Put on your big girl pants and go over there. You need to bust out of your comfort zone."

My eyes glued to the wood counter, I twisted my hands in the folds of the dress. I wasn't prepared to meet a man like him today. Who was I kidding? I'd never be prepared, and that thought coupled with too much alcohol made me a little reckless. "What the hell," I said. I slid off the raised surface and pushed through the masses of people.

"You've got this," Vera shouted after me, but I didn't turn around to acknowledge her comment. I would catch up with her in a few minutes after I crashed and burned because there wasn't any other possibility. I shoved my way through the crowd, brushing up against undulating bodies, a few wandering hands, and a whole lot of sweaty skin.

When the crowd cleared, I came face to face with him. I blinked, overwhelmed and wide-eyed. Close up, he was downright intimidating and a million times more devastatingly handsome than from afar. He was a little older than me, but he had every physical characteristic a woman wanted in a man: broad shoulders, powerfully sculpted muscles, dark hair just long enough to curl at the ends, and a savagely elegant face that hinted at a thinly concealed eroticism. At this range, I even saw his eyes. They were a striking shade of gray that both complemented and enhanced his olive complexion, and they were trained 100 percent on me.

Sure, I had encountered many powerful and attractive men in my life. After all, my dad was the Attorney General of the United States, which was a big deal. Interacting with the political elite was just another day on the playground for me, but none of them compared to this man. Not even close. Power, control, and something intangible seeped from him in wicked abundance.

I opened my mouth, but nothing came out. I

didn't move. I didn't blink. Apparently, my brain had disconnected from my mouth and my body. Even with the aid of Vera's little pep talks, I crashed and burned the second I came face to face with Mr. Dark and Sexy. Game over. There was no way in hell I could talk to him, much less use him as an Evan mind eraser. I pivoted backward, determined to flee.

"Are you going to talk to me or did I already scare you away?" His voice whispered down my spine, and the hair on my forearms stood on end. The glint in his eyes said things that his mouth hadn't, or maybe my overactive imagination needed to shut the hell up.

"Um…" My mind scrambled into a million puzzle pieces, and then I found my voice. "No. I'd like another drink." I pointed with a limp finger toward the bar, horrified by my attempt at making conversation.

Satisfaction slid across his face. He knew I wasn't leaving. "I can help you with that." He lifted two fingers and motioned for the bartender. Less than five seconds later, the bartender hovered in front of him expectantly. All night, Vera and I had to flash our breasts to elicit his attention. Not really, but close. "Another Prairie Fire or a Red Headed Slut? Maybe something different this time?" He raised one dark, perfectly arched eyebrow, humor lighting the sharp angles of his face.

Vera was right. He had been watching me all night. I couldn't decide if that was a good thing, but I elected to stay the course for a few minutes and feel him out. "You pick."

His lips hinted at a lopsided smile, and my heart nearly exploded in my chest. A direct hit to my heart would have been less effective. "Two glasses of Patron on the rocks with a splash of soda water."

"No fancy name for that drink?" I asked rocking back on my heels.

"Not everything needs a name." He leaned closer to the man next to him and whispered something next his ear. The man immediately vacated his seat.

"Sit." He motioned toward the empty chair...another thing I hadn't been able to score tonight.

"I'm Hattie." I slipped into the seat next to him, my body a foot away from him, but still too close for my comfort.

"Hattie," he repeated. The way my name rolled over his tongue was more intoxicating than my last few shots. "That's an interesting name."

"My mom named me after Hattie Caraway—the first woman elected to a full term in the U.S. Senate."

"Does that mean you have political aspirations?"

"My mom wants me to be involved in politics." My dad held all the political clout in their relationship and she resented him for it. She didn't want that for me. She wanted me to be the person with the power. She met my dad at Harvard Law School, but she dropped out when she got pregnant with my brother. She has never let me forget she considers that decision her biggest mistake.

"I'm Ryker." He pushed my hair behind my ears and with one delicate stroke, the air evaporated from my lungs. Caught in the tangle of his sea gray eyes, I leaned forward, dropping my gaze to his lips.

I bit my lower lip. "What brings you to the bar tonight?"

"A drink. What about you?" Ryker asked.

"Boredom and peer pressure," I responded.

Ryker's lips quirked up at the corners. "Maybe I could help you relieve some of your boredom."

I narrowed my eyes. "Oh really, and what would you suggest?"

Ryker slid my drink across the bar countertop toward me. "A drink. Conversation. Maybe more."

I swallowed hard, trying to beat back the anxiety bubbling in my stomach. "Why don't we start with the drink and conversation?" I lifted my glass and took a healthy gulp of my drink.

He stared at me, burning up my insides with a predatory gaze. His eyes swept down my body, lingering on the deep "v" of my dress, sending a tingling sensation straight to my core before his eyes met mine again. "Fine. If that makes you comfortable, I don't mind pretending we don't know the end game…at least for a little while. We'll finish our drink first. "

My hand froze; drink in hand, halfway to my mouth. I stared at him, my lips parted, my breathing accelerated as his words washed over me. Panic, astonishment, and excitement swirled inside of me. Conflicting urges to flee or drag him back to my hotel room warred inside my body. Both thoughts seemed ridiculous. Weighing my options, I shifted to the end of my seat. "What's the end game?" I asked, my throat dry and a bit shaky.

He leaned forward trailing a fingertip along my

jaw line. "We can sit here and have a friendly chat, but we both know that this night ends with me buried inside of you." He cocked his head to the side. "I'm hoping it happens sooner rather than later, though," he said, lowering his voice to a wicked drawl.

Who said shit like that? I snickered trying to lighten the mood, but it didn't help. Desire brewed in the air around us, making it impossible to ignore him. I drew in a forceful breath as my eyes flittered around the bar, searching for Vera. Normally, she stood out like a beacon in a sea of blonde and brown, but I didn't see her long, flowing red mane anywhere.

"She disappeared toward the beach with a man a few minutes ago." Ryker waved his hand in the direction of the long span of doors open to beach at back of the bar.

"Vera?"

"Is that her name?"

I nodded as I swallowed nervously. "Why are you interested in me?" It was a dumb question, but the thought tumbled from my mouth before I stopped it. I wasn't ugly, but I didn't draw the attention of many men either. Vera does…not me.

Secrets danced behind his guarded eyes, but Ryker didn't answer. He snagged my hand and pulled me off my chair. A heated, tingling current traveled the length of my arm, but I didn't have the time to analyze it. Instinctively, I tensed for a beat, pulling back…resisting him, but he didn't release my hand. He pulled me closer until his hard chest whispered a darkly suggestive promise against mine.

"Let's dance," he said, his lips only millimeters from my bare skin. Shivers cascaded down my neck, and my heart sputtered. I was enthralled, spellbound, and already dancing to his seductive tune.

Even as I followed him into the maze of people, I knew I shouldn't go anywhere with him, but when I gazed into his smoky gray eyes, I buried my better judgment into the recesses of my mind. At twenty-four years old, I needed to start living my life for me instead of my family. And right now, that included doing things I had every intention of blaming on the ignorance of youth.

# Chapter Six

In the middle of the dance floor, he circled his arms around me, pulling my body flush against his. My silky black dress didn't offer much of a barrier between his body and mine. The fevered glide of my skin against his black cotton shirt and his muscular thighs as we moved to the beat felt good. Better than good. Fucking amazing. I inwardly heckled myself for my inappropriate behavior even as I slid closer. I wanted to sink into him, embrace the moment. What harm could come of it?

In a foreign country, in the arms of a stranger with no familiar faces to judge my actions and report my unbecoming behavior, I decided to live. Fuck Evan and all his apologies that filled my phone on a daily basis. My mom, my brother, my friends…everyone except Vera wanted me to give Evan another chance. They reminded me of Evan's promising future career in politics at every turn. His dad was a U.S. Senator, and Evan probably would be one someday too. If I married Evan after everything he'd done, it'd be a political merger, nothing more. Evan didn't love me…he never did. I realized that now. You didn't lie and cheat when you loved someone.

Ryker's hand coasted down my spine, resting at my lower back, and I arched into him, our hips moving in perfect synchronicity with the beat of the music. My hands wandered up the sculpted planes of his chest, and I feathered soft kisses along his neck. He smelled like a mixture of masculine spice and salty sea air.

My actions were stupid. I meant to tease him…control him, but he had other plans. One of his hands traced the outline of my body from my waist to the subtle curve of my breast. His thumb grazed the tip of one nipple then the other, making them so hard they throbbed within the confines of my black lace bra. When I thought I'd melt into a puddle of need, his hands glided around my hips, guiding my movements, grinding his pelvis against mine, and I was the one being tortured.

He tipped my chin up, and the flashing lights of the bar lit the sharp angled planes of his face, accentuating his devastating beauty. The full effect of his smoky gaze pierced through me, enslaving me, mesmerizing me. A shot of adrenaline coursed like wildfire through my body as our connection simmered to a full boil.

I whimpered, but he halted the release of my breath with the press of his thumb against my parted mouth. His thumb traced the contour of my lips, likely smearing Vera's magic red lipstick, but I didn't care. I was under his spell—compliant, willing, my eyes begging for things my mouth wouldn't. I nipped the tip of his thumb and his eyes darkened. "See? I warned you this is where the night would go."

Before his comment invaded the haze of lust overwhelming my senses, his hand cupped my chin, and his lips crashed against mine. His kiss was far from gentle, but I didn't care. I matched him stroke for stroke, bite for bite, and losing touch with reality under the whirlwind of his assault.

Every contour of his body belonged to me at that instant, and I intended to take advantage of it. My hands darted under his shirt, roaming along the hard planes of his chest and stomach.

His hand skated up my thigh, cupping my sex in the middle of the dance floor. Common sense told me to object, but my mind was blind, deaf, and dumb to anything but him and the sensations rolling through me. Greedy, eager gasps fell from my mouth as his hand rubbed against my mound. I wanted to use him…steal every inch of him and burn the memories into my mind for later when my mom managed to marry me off to Evan or his stuffy clone.

His hand slipped into my panties, and my breath rushed out in a needy moan. With every slip, slide, and caress of his finger, flames licked at my body until it practically hummed. Instinctively, I wrapped my leg around his waist, grinding against him. Ryker nipped my lower lip, and my knees buckled as seeds of an explosive orgasm spread from my core up the length of my spine. Like Houdini, he made everything beyond the two of us evaporate. I probably wouldn't have resisted if he spread me out on the dirty, sticky floor and fucked me in front of hundreds of strangers.

I palmed his erection through his pants, wildly seeking evidence that he felt this...that he needed this. Insane or not, I needed to feel this stranger inside of me. *Wow*. I didn't even recognize my lusty mind.

Ryker sucked in a weighted breath. "Not here." His voice mimicked gravel against satin, but it called out to me like nothing I'd ever heard. Distantly, I pondered why everything sounded better, sexier, and infinitely hotter coming out of his sultry, made for sin mouth. Who the fuck was this man? He scattered my thoughts and turned me into liquid fire within minutes...no, seconds.

His hand coiled around mine, biting into the fragile bones of my hand. Too mindless to object, I followed blindly in pursuit of the sexual emancipation written in every ruthless curve of his face.

Less than a minute later, we were outside the bar. The humid air ruffled through my hair, lifting it from my shoulders and whipping it around my face. Music from the nightclubs dueled for the attention of the tourists strolling the sidewalks in a drunken fog. But none of that registered in my mind. Alcohol and single-minded lust surged through my veins, clouding my vision until I couldn't think of anything but the release Ryker promised.

He pulled me along the side of a darkened building, an alley of sorts, and pressed me against the wall. A thrill skittered down my spine as the stucco bit into my back and snagged the silken weave of my little black dress.

Less than a beat later, he pressed his body against mine as his hands hiked up the bottom of my dress. The humid, tropical air hummed around my sensitive skin, and I ached for him. I pulled his face to mine, sucking his tongue into my mouth. He tasted of tequila and sin, and I wanted more. I demanded more.

Not wasting a second, his finger slid inside of me, and he groaned into my mouth, igniting pleasure-laced vibrations in my already pulsing core. "You're so wet," he said as his lips ghosted along my neck, my pulse a rapid staccato under his wandering mouth.

"Mm," I moaned, grinding my pelvis against his hand. My hands fumbled with his belt buckle. I was done with foreplay. Game over. I wanted him inside of me. Now.

"Fuck," he said ripping my hands away just as I managed to release his buckle. He pulled a small square package out of his pocket.

I both loved and hated that he had a condom. Loved because I wanted him buried inside me with as little to regret as possible tomorrow. Hated because it made me realize he might do this often. I forced the thought from my mind. None of that mattered. I had no intention of seeing Ryker after tonight. He'd be my dirty secret...one huge silent fuck you to my mom, Evan, and the next guy my parents shoved in my face when they finally accepted I wouldn't rekindle my relationship with Evan.

With unsteady hands, I released his button and

his zipper. He shoved his pants and boxer briefs down his hips just far enough to free himself, but not far enough to expose himself to wandering eyes. Within seconds, he rolled a condom over his erection. A quick snap of his hand and my panties were discarded in a mystery puddle near our feet.

He wrapped one of my legs around his waist, spreading me, revealing me, and he plunged inside with one deep, breath-robbing thrust. His eyes never left mine as he pounded into me with a confidence and skill I'd never experienced.

In.

Out.

And back in again.

Deeper and harder with every jutting stroke of his hips.

My senses whirled and faded into the moment, unable to concentrate on anything but the building pressure as he moved inside me.

Twisting his fingers into my hair, he gripped my head, his hands biting into my cheeks, his eyes devouring me. The sharp bite of pain only enhanced my desire.

With his gray eyes boring into mine, I imagined he saw through me, penetrating the deep recesses of my mind where I buried secrets, lies, and all the insecurities locked inside my soul. It was too much. I didn't want an emotional connection. I wanted a mindless fuck that transported me out of my self-induced agony and pity into a mind-shattering pleasure so raw and deep I'd never forget it. Shaking out of his clasp, I dropped my head and closed my eyes, concentrating on the delicious bite of his cock and the rattling of my teeth as he slammed into me.

Without words, he complied, shoving me harder into the wall. His hands tore at my dress. When the material buckled under his strength, he raked the soft skin of my breasts with his hand. I'd never experienced anything so rough and mindless. My perfectly tailored life faded into a blur of primal bliss. I liked it. No, I fucking loved it.

He lifted my other leg, his hands digging into the flesh of my ass, and just like that, an incoherent, disconnected sound escaped my mouth as the most insanely mind-numbing orgasm slashed through my body. A dark tide of pleasure swallowed me as I screamed, unconcerned with who heard. Like a savage, my nails clawed at the hard planes of his shoulders and any other body part I could find, trying to pull him deeper into me…into this chasm of soulless rapture.

"Fuck," he yelled as he pounded into me. My head hit the wall, and my eyes connected with his at the exact instant of his release. Brutal pleasure contorted the angular features of his face into something both beautiful and wicked.

Then, everything stopped and he froze inside me. The pounding of the music, the low hum of conversation, and the bursts of laughter seeped back into my reality. Out of breath, he buried his head against my shoulder as he released my shaky legs.

With my mind luxuriating in the fog of sex, he tangled one of his hands into my hair and forced me to look at him. Everything was blurred, softer, happier…disguising the hard truths of what just happened. I preferred it. I embraced it. No regrets. A languid smile pulled at the edge my lips. My body wanted him again and again.

"Sorry," he murmured, his gray eyes simmering with regret. I didn't understand what he meant, and I opened my mouth to ask, but without warning, a sharp object pierced the thin skin of my neck.

He brushed a kiss across my lips, and my brain became fuzzier and fuzzier as one second bled into the next. Nothing made sense, but then my body swayed and an instant of absolute clarity flashed through my mind.

"You drugged me. Why?" I whispered, my tongue thick and heavy as it rolled over the words in my mouth.

"Because you're you," he whispered as my vision faded into nothingness.

# Chapter Seven

*Present Day*

It had been hours since Ryker walked out of the room without explaining anything, leaving me tied to a wooden chair. The room didn't have a single window, picture, or piece of furniture, except for the chair I sat on and a long wooden table behind me. The silence in the room was deafening; even my breath and the quiet hum of the florescent light seemed loud.

I stared at the white walls and the gray concrete floors as my mind stalked one horrible scenario after another, each worse than the previous. Deviants kept women chained to the walls. Religious fanatics groomed women to be subservient slaves. Sex traffickers drugged women and sold them. Serial murderers abducted women and tortured and killed them. I took a deep breath and closed my eyes, trying to beat back my impending panic attack.

I concentrated on the tangible items connecting me to that point in time just like my childhood therapist taught me. My chair was wood. The walls were white. My feet touched the concrete floor. The coarse hairs of the rope chaffed my skin. My bladder was insanely full. Slowly, my heartbeat returned to normal.

Just as the pressure building in my bladder had become too much, and I decided I didn't care if I soiled myself, the door opened behind me. My muscles coiled into knots waiting for a word. None were spoken. Instead, I listened to the soft shuffle of leather shoes over concrete and faint inhalations and exhalations, moving closer and closer with each passing second.

I could have said something, but I didn't. I didn't have anything to say, not yet anyway, and screaming wouldn't help. I screamed after Ryker left for so long that my throat felt as though I had just finished my first performance as a fire swallower.

"Are you hungry?"

Ryker. I couldn't see his face, but I didn't need to. I recognized his voice. He placed his hands on my shoulders, his front to my back. I could smell him—spice mixed with salty sea air. Fear and loathing in the form of a shudder crept down my spine.

I shook my head.

"Thirsty?" He squeezed my shoulders.

I nodded. I was so fucking thirsty I couldn't form the words. I wanted to be strong and refuse anything from him, but I was weak in both my mind and body. Unless I did something about it, I'd become progressively weaker with every passing hour. My throat throbbed. My eyes were so dry that I heard the clicking sound of my eyelids as they slid over my eyeball with every blink. My skull pounded.

He removed his hands from my shoulders, and I blew out a huge breath, lifting my heavy bangs from my forehead. I tried to ignore it, but I could still feel the imprint of his hands on my shoulders. Less than a minute later, he crouched down in front of me, a plastic cup filled with a clear liquid in one hand.

I glared pointedly at my bindings. "Are you going to untie me?" The words came out as a strangled whisper.

He smiled a faint, maddening grin that mocked my very existence. "No."

One fucking word. "Are you going dump it over my face or make me lap it up like a dog?"

"No." He lifted the glass to my lips, and I greedily sucked the liquid into my Sahara-like mouth.

"More?" he asked when he pulled it away.

I tipped up my chin. "You won't get away with this. Vera knows I left with you."

He cocked his head to the side, watching me carefully, completely unmoved by my words. Calm amusement lit the savage planes of his face. "No. She knows you talked to a guy at a bar, but she left before we danced or even before you sat down. I made sure of it. I don't make mistakes. No one can trace you to me." His lips curved in a smile that was miles from reassuring. "Besides, this is Mexico. The bureaucratic red tape between here and your government will give me months of lead time."

In one sickening rush, my stomach caved in on

itself and the water I drank threatened to reverse its course as I processed his words. "You sent that man to talk to Vera to get rid of her so you could…" I gasped, and the blood drained from my face, leaving me lightheaded. He set me up. He planned everything. This wasn't a random crime of opportunity. This was much worse. He had targeted me.

"I've been watching you for a while." He stood up, and I hated the lethal grace oozing out of him. I hated I even noticed, but his magnetic charm wouldn't fool me today. Without alcohol flowing through my veins, he looked dangerous, but maybe that was just my imagination. A black shirt stretched across his chest. The stubble on his face was thicker and blacker than last night, but he was just a man, even if my mind wanted to believe otherwise.

I bit my lower lip until the faint, metallic taste of blood flavored my saliva. "Are you going to kill me?"

"I don't think it will come to that." His voice was casual, lazy even, but his eyes weren't. His gray irises focused on me with hyper-vigilance.

My eyes flared, and blood roared through my head, compounding the paralyzing effect of last night's alcoholic binge and whatever drug Ryker used to sedate me. "What's that supposed to mean?"

He shoved his hands into his pockets, his face entirely too blank for my comfort. "As long as your father does what he's told, you should be home before the end of next week."

The tension twisting my muscles into frozen

knots, released just a fraction. I had faith in my dad. He would do whatever it took to extract me from this hellhole. He may not be the best parent in the world, but he took care of his family. He loved me even if he was absent more often than not. Unlike the rest of my family, he hadn't pressured me to work things out with Evan. "What's he supposed to do?"

"Pardon my brother."

"Who's your brother?"

"Rever Vargas."

My mind raced through the back alleys of my brain trying to place the name, but nothing came to me. I shook my head, a fresh wave of agony radiating through my skull. "What makes him so important?"

Ryker laughed, a quiet and unsettling sound. "He's my father's son."

"Who's your father?"

"Ignacio Vargas."

A little flutter of something—maybe a memory—rushed through my brain, but nothing of substance and nothing identifiable. "So." I tried to shrug, but the ropes binding me to the chair bit in my wrists.

He caught my chin between his thumb and his index finger, and an unhurried, enigmatic, and impossibly sexy smile tugged on the corners of his lips. I wanted to hit him. He leaned toward me, and I considered spitting in his face, but he pressed his finger to my mouth. "Don't try it," he warned, his voice deadly calm, his eyes an opaque, impenetrable mask.

I glared at him, summoning years of anger, frustration, and hatred into the narrowing of my eyes. He bent closer, his lips within striking distance of mine, and for one terrifying second, I thought he'd kiss me. But instead, he yanked his finger from my lips and stood up in one fluid movement. Without looking back, he stalked toward the door, his heavy footsteps echoing through the empty room.

"Wait," I yelled, craning my head to the side as far as humanly possible. "I need to go to the bathroom."

He paused, but he didn't respond.

"And I'd like a change of clothes," I added. Ryker had torn the strap on my dress last night, and I hated the memory of that moment glaring at me, taunting me with my impulsive stupidity.

"Fine," he answered in his smooth, velvety voice. The door slammed, and it took less than a second for the tears mixed with semi-hysterical hiccups to surface.

I shouldn't have gone on this trip. I should've got back together with Evan, the self-absorbed asshole. I should've refused to go to the bar with Vera. I wished I never touched Ryker. Shame and cruel self-loathing rushed hot and cold through my veins as visions of Ryker and me on the dance floor and in the alley flashed through my mind. I enjoyed having sex with a monster, which clearly meant something was wrong with me.

I didn't even hear the door open again. I was too busy floating in a haze of self-pity and regret. The ropes slackened around my wrists and then my ankles, and Ryker's arms wrapped around my waist pulling me up. Pins and needles of pain shot through my limbs as blood rushed into my starved fingers and toes. I would've collapsed if it weren't for Ryker.

"There's a bathroom down the hall on the right. You need to be quiet and listen to everything I say. If you try to run or attack me, you won't like the consequences." His words were harsh, and the frozen mask of fury on his face told me he meant it.

I nodded, unable and unwilling to form words of gratitude or anger. He restrained my hands behind my back with one hand. He placed his other hand around the front of my neck, warning me what would happen if I tried to resist or escape.

I stumbled as he muscled me into a small, dark room and then flipped on the lights. The room had a toilet, a cabinet with a sink, a square mirror, and a small shower stall. Everything was white with concrete floors just like the room where Ryker held me captive.

He pulled a robe from underneath the sink and draped it over a hook next to the shower. "You can shower and use the bathroom," he said as he folded his arms across his chest, leaning against the door.

I snatched the robe off the hook. "Are you staying?"

"Can I trust you not to run?"

"No," I shot back before I contemplated the consequences of my answer. *Dumbass*.

"Then I'll wait here. Go ahead." He nodded his head in the direction of the shower.

"No," I shouted. My heart seized with a

sickening terror. I imagined his silvery eyes crawling over my naked body. Enough guilt and self-hatred already assaulted my conscience for having sex with him. I didn't need any more.

He rolled his eyes. "For fuck's sake, Hattie, I have no interest in your naked body or touching any part of you. There's no need to be modest." His eyes danced with amusement like he found the whole situation hilarious, and it stung for too many reasons to contemplate.

Asshole.

Asshole.

Asshole.

Humiliation heated my cheekbones and quickly spread down my face to my neck. "Then, why'd you touch me last night?" My voice was so small and pathetic I wanted to shrink into nothingness and disappear. His words plunged into my heart like an invisible spear. Logically, why he fucked me wasn't important. It happened. Given the chance, I'd rewind history. Regrets were a waste of time and brainpower. Unfortunately, my emotional mind snubbed my rational mind.

His eyebrows lifted, his eyes void of all emotion once again. "It was my job to procure you by any means necessary. You were open to sex, so that's the tool I used." He crossed his ankles and the corners of his mouth twitched. "It worked."

My mouth opened and then closed quickly as my mind spun in circles. I pinched the bridge of my nose trying to find balance and calm. I took a deep breath, and resignation settled into my bones. I wanted to be clean and wash every ounce of him from my body. Then, I'd regroup and figure out how to sneak away from him. "Fine," I whispered, turning my back to him and pulling the tattered remains of my dress over my head. I crumbled it into a ball and tossed it in the trashcan next to the sink. At least the tiny shower stall had a curtain rather than glass.

I stepped into the shower and turned it on full force. Ice-cold water ran down my skin and I gasped. Numb with defeat, I didn't care. I stood there with my eyes closed, frozen and shivering under the stream of water until the temperature adjusted.

I didn't know how much time had passed when the shower curtain scraped across the rusted metal bar. I flinched, but kept my eyes closed choosing to ignore reality. Ryker pulled my body toward the opening. "Don't."

"I'm going to wash you."

"No." My eyes popped open, and I ripped the bar of soap out of his hands. "I don't want you to touch me."

"Fine." His face impassive, his voice bland, he drew the shower curtain closed. "Do it yourself, but be quick because you only have two more minutes. I'm done playing games with you. I have shit to do today that doesn't involve pampering a worthless socialite."

My hand contracted around the soap so hard I thought it'd crumble, and at that moment I made myself a promise. I'd eat. I'd drink. I'd tell him and anyone else what they wanted to hear. I'd learn his vulnerabilities. I'd be totally compliant, but the minute Ryker's watchfulness faltered, I'd fucking run and I'd be free. I didn't brush up against the masters of manipulation my entire life without learning more than I'd ever wanted to know about survival and deceit.

# Chapter Eight

"Here's where you'll live for the next few weeks." Ryker threw open a white steel door.

I tightened the belt on my robe as my eyes scanned the room. No window. White walls. Narrow bed. White coverlet. White linens. Painted white concrete floors. I always liked the perceived elegance and simplicity of white, but right then I promised myself a life full of color when I escaped. Not if, but when, because there wasn't an alternative. I refused to die at the age of twenty-four in the middle of nowhere before I had the opportunity to do anything with my life. And when I got my life back, I wouldn't cave to my parents' demands or expectations…ever.

"It's like my private padded cell minus the padding," I mumbled under my breath. If he heard me, he didn't care.

"Most of the items from your suitcase are on the shelves in the closet." His arm waved in the direction of the door at the far end of the room.

"Most?" I questioned, brushing my damp hair

behind my ears.

"I discarded anything that you might use to harm yourself or us."

"Us?" I glanced over my shoulder.

"Yes." He chuckled. "There are others."

"How flattering," I mocked, flinging myself onto the narrow bed. Unfortunately, it was as hard as it looked and nearly knocked the air from my lungs when I landed. "An entire team of deranged assholes all dedicated to restraining a hundred and fifteen pound woman."

"Someone will bring you food within an hour." He smirked. "It's probably not what you're used to, but I think you'll you find it acceptable."

"I'll be fine. I don't care what I eat."

Ignoring the plastic chair in the corner, he reclined on the edge of my bed, his long muscular legs stretching out in from of him. I wished he would move. Up close, he was just as mesmerizing as the first time my eyes connected with his last night. I didn't want him to lull me into a false sense of security.

"So who do you think will come to your rescue? Your dad or your lover's family?"

My brow furrowed. "How do you know about Evan?"

He shrugged. "I know a lot of things."

My body stiffened. "How?"

His lips curled into a slow, unsettling, almost predatory smile. Vivid, heated images of his lips exploring mine flashed through my mind. Shame raced through my body. I jerked my head to the side, closing my eyes, trying to erase the image

59

from my mind.

He trailed his finger down the exposed flesh of my thigh. My stomach twisted in knots.

"Do you think Evan would still want you if he knew you spread your legs for me?"

I covered my face with my hands, but a rough-edged sob escaped my mouth. It didn't matter what he said. I didn't care.

He peeled my hands from my face, tilting my chin, forcing me to look at him with his icy gray eyes. He leaned toward me, his body braced above mine. "Don't look so stricken. Maybe he wouldn't care." One side of his mouth lifted. "He has some unusual tastes, but you don't know that yet, do you? He usually goes elsewhere for those needs."

He said it to bait me. I wasn't dumb. I realized that, but for some reason my mind wasn't 100 percent sure he had lied. I knew Evan cheated. I saw it. He admitted to it and more, but maybe Evan held something back. Something darker. Something unforgivable.

A tear rolled down my face, but not because I still loved Evan. I didn't. I wasn't sure I ever did, but Ryker had kicked me in the gut while I was down. "Given that we broke up weeks ago, what Evan likes is no longer relevant," I said, my voice choked and shaky, instead of unconcerned and confident as I intended. I cleared my throat. "I will never get back together with him. Never."

"Really? Are you sure about that?" He raised one eyebrow, his jaw clenched and his lips pressed into a tight line.

I hit him hard in the middle of his chest with my

palm, shoving him backward and out of my space. I searched his intense face, and then it hit me. He didn't know I broke up with Evan. He wanted Evan to care, to be franticly searching for his lost love. Unbidden, a bitter laugh spilled from my mouth as tears rained down my face. One point for me. "You couldn't have been watching me very closely if you missed that fact. Everyone knows I caught him cheating on me. I guess you don't know as much as you think you do."

He stood up. "Hopefully he still cares enough to help you. Senator Deveron would be a useful ally. If not, you'll only have one person to dissect the months of red tape to pardon my brother and secure your release. You might not make it that long." He stalked toward the door.

"Maybe your brother won't either."

"I'm not worried. The U.S. government doesn't torture its prisoners, especially a high profile one with useful connections and information." He shrugged and glanced over his shoulder, his silver eyes glowing with a sinister light. "I can't say the same about the Vargas Cartel."

My mind swirled as he slammed the door and locked it, cutting me off from the world. Not that there was much to see and explore outside my white prison cell, but I hated being alone. I hated silence more, and it appeared I'd have a heavy dose of both in the foreseeable future. The soft hum of silence reminded me of a lifetime of disapproval when I didn't wear the right outfit, say the right thing, or eat the right food. From an early age, those all too frequent occasions always ended the same way…with me alone in my room contemplating how I would do better next time.

As I opened the closet, I found a small stack of clothing. Dropping my robe on the floor, I pulled a dress over my head. I didn't know much about the Vargas Cartel, just a few tidbits of information from my Latin American politics class.

From what I recalled, they controlled the vast stretch of land from Nuevo Leon, which bordered Texas, all the way south to the Yucatan—which included my vacation destination. From all accounts, the Vargas Cartel had a distinguished record as drug traffickers, human traffickers, arms traffickers, highly efficient executors…and those were just the offenses I remembered off the top of my head. They were equal opportunity players, ruthlessly diving into anything that made money. According to some experts, their range of influence extended to the U.S.

I sank down onto the floor next to the bed, dropping my head into my shaky hands. I was fucked. Of all the places in the world where Vera could have convinced me to go for Spring Break, she'd picked an area associated with the Vargas Cartel. Instead of taking a vacation to escape my nagging parents and Evan's pathetic apologies, I had taken a vacation to the center of hell with little hope of escape.

How would my dad get me out of this mess? Miles of red tape stood in the way of my release. Securing Rever Vargas's release wouldn't be easy either. My dad would have to call in every political favor in his arsenal and then some. The U.S.

government rarely negotiated with criminal organizations and terrorists, which sounded like a good policy until it directly impacted me.

Even if my dad succeeded, I still might not make it out of this mess alive. Every day I spent as a prisoner of the Vargas Cartel increased the chances that I'd learn too much and inadvertently sign my death warrant.

# Chapter Nine

When I crawled into the small bed, I knew I'd never be able to fall asleep. Every inch of my body vibrated with anger. I wanted to tear apart the room and turn it upside down. My wrists, ankles, and head throbbed in unison. I should have begged for food when I had the chance. My stomach felt sunken and nauseous—a combination of too little food, too much alcohol, and the lingering effects of whatever Ryker injected into my neck.

I heard a click at my door, and I shot up in bed. A man I didn't recognize walked through the door carrying a tray of food. Without a word, he sat it on the edge of the bed. Unlike Ryker, he wasn't tall. In fact, he was probably a good three inches shorter than me. He wore a white collared shirt and tan pants. He had dark hair and wide-set eyes, and black tattoos covering both of his arms.

"I'm not hungry," I shouted at him, despite the relentless growling and churning of my stomach.

He cocked his head to the side but didn't say anything.

"How long do I have to stay in this room?"

Again, he didn't answer.

Frustration boiled under my skin. I picked up the bottle of water on the tray and tossed at the wall, grazing the side of the man's head. "Can't you talk or is your silence part of the plan to torture me?"

His lips drew back over his yellowed teeth, and he stalked toward me, his entire body rigid. He had an odd, jittery intensity that caused the hair on my arms to rise in protest. Confused, I took a few steps backward until my back hit the cold, cement wall. I lunged sideways, but his hand encircled the base of my throat, the pressure enough to restrict, but not sever the airflow to my lungs. His fingers bit into my skin.

"I can hear you," he barked through clenched teeth, a faint accent flavoring his words. "But I don't give a fuck what you have to say or what you want. If it were up to me, you'd be dead, *puta.*" His breath smelled of onions and garlic, and I shifted my head to the side, but he snapped my head forward, forcing me to look at him.

His pupils contracted to a black pinpoint, and the hand on my neck tightened until edges of my vision blurred. Woozy, I shook my head wildly from side to side as tears rolled freely down my cheeks. "I'm sorry. Let me go," I said, but the words were garbled and meaningless to him.

Desperately trying to free my neck from his grip, my fingers clawed at his hand without success. A harsh, sinister laugh erupted from his mouth, and he lifted a shiny, short blade in front of my face, twirling it back and forth, taunting me. Then, he trailed it down my cheek, along my neck to the hollow at the base of my throat. Even though he didn't puncture my skin, my heart pounded so hard, I thought it'd rip through the walls of my chest.

With soulless, vacant eyes, he sliced one strap of my sundress and then the other. His hand pressed even tighter around my neck, and I wondered if this was how I would die…at the hands of a nameless man, in a nondescript room, my body buried somewhere in the Yucatan jungle. With one final burst of effort, I tried to lift my leg to knee him in the balls, but the muscles in my legs refused to cooperate. They were boneless, collapsing under the weight of my body held up only by the press of his hand.

Suddenly, the door flew opened so hard it rebounded and almost closed again. With gray eyes the color of thunderclouds, Ryker stalked through the door, his hands fisted at his sides, color staining his cheeks.

One.

Two.

Three steps and he stood next to me, hovering over us like an avenging specter. Not wasting a second, he yanked the man's hands from my neck. Like a lifeless doll, I collapsed to my knees, bracing my throbbing neck with my fingers and gasping for air.

Ryker shoved the man into the wall, his hand fisted in the man's shirt. *"¿Qué mierda estás haciendo?"*

*"Ella arrojó una botella hacia mi cabeza. Tienes suerte que no la maté,"* the nameless man spat, his

face the color of molten lava, his eyes flashing, and his hands fisted in the material of his tan pants.

"*No importa*," Ryker yelled, along with hundreds of other words I couldn't begin to understand. He repeatedly slammed the stranger into the wall, punctuating each sentence or thought with the thud of flesh hitting cement.

My mind swirled watching the exchange of rapid-fire Spanish. I took three years of Spanish in high school, and I recognized a few words, but not enough to decipher the conversation. I heard *kill*, *head,* and *bottle,* but the other words meant nothing.

I should have screamed or ran. Instead, I sat unmoving as tremors ravaged my limbs, and air slowly refueled my oxygen-deprived body.

"Find someone else to babysit her," the man screamed, switching to English as he flung his hand toward me.

"*Déjanos!*" Ryker tossed the man toward the door by his shirt.

The door to the bedroom slammed shut, echoing off the barren walls and concrete floors. Ryker turned his back to me, his hands buried deep in the pockets of his jeans, and his head bent. Shouts in Spanish and loud crashes filtered through the heavy door.

When the voices stopped, Ryker turned, crouching down in front of me. Breathing heavily, he grazed my neck with his fingertips. I recoiled, not wanting to be touched by him or anybody else. My hands shaking, I jammed my fist into my mouth, suddenly overwhelmed by the reality of my situation. A brutal cartel had drugged and abducted me. I'd be lucky if I walked away from this situation with my life, because I was starting to realize my only way out might be in a body bag.

"Stop," he whispered, his voice raw. "I need to check your injuries."

"I'm fine, not that you care." I crab-walked backward, but I didn't get far before the cold wall pressed into my back, trapping me.

"No, you're not fine, and your condition definitely matters," he said gruffly as he wrapped his arms around me and lifted me from the ground. I kicked him. I elbowed him and pulled at his hair. Nothing worked. He restrained me with minimal effort. The hard planes of his chest were warm against the front of my body, and his heart drummed wildly against his ribcage, which seemed wrong. He should feel icy, cold, and inhuman, because he was. He was a criminal.

Ryker dumped me on the bed. "What the hell?"

*Shit.* Tears rushed down my face, mingling with the snot from my nose. If I could see myself I'd be horrified, but I didn't have the luxury of caring about my appearance any longer. I just needed him to leave. I tried to shield my face from him, but he snatched my hands, pressing them into the rock hard mattress as his eyes surveyed every inch of my body. I closed my eyes, unable to witness his icy perusal as though I were an inanimate object.

After seconds that stretched like hours, he released my hands and I rolled to my side, my back to him.

The bed dipped behind me, and he rested his hand on my hip. "You need to eat."

"For some unfathomable reason, I lost my appetite." I kicked the tray, but it only budged an inch or two.

"Nobody wants to see you hurt. As long as the U.S. government releases my brother, I'm happy to let you go. In fact, I'll fly you first-class back to the U.S."

I rolled onto my back and stroked the tender skin of my neck. It'd be black and blue soon if it weren't already. "You could've fooled me."

His lips pressed into a firm line, and he sighed in exasperation. "Just behave yourself and this whole thing will be infinitely easier for you. Don't make waves."

Did he think I was stupid? I couldn't believe any word that tumbled from his beautifully cruel lips. "Just let me go and I'll talk to my dad. I'll convince him to grant a pardon for your brother or whatever the hell else you want. I have to go home." My heart pounded against the walls of my chest. "I have to be in school in a couple days. I can't miss. I'm a teaching assistant. I have a few more months until graduation. I have an internship lined up this summer."

He slanted forward so his mouth was less than an inch from my ear. "Sorry, Hattie," he murmured in a soft, soothing voice. "But I can't have you complicating my plans. When Rever's released, you'll be released. Tit for tat. And even if I wanted to let you go, I couldn't."

"Sorry?" I shook my head from side to side, strands of hair whipping across my face. "Sorry for what? Abducting me? Imprisoning me? Drugging

69

me? Fucking me in a dirty alley?"

A faint chuckled escaped his lips. "If I said all of the above, would you be happy? Or maybe I should apologize for everything but fucking you." He cocked his head to the side, and a lock of midnight colored hair veiled his expressive eyebrows. "My memory is hazy, but I think you enjoyed it."

I gasped. Satisfaction curled his lips into a wicked smile, and my stomach rolled in giant waves. "Shut up. Just shut up. You're an asshole."

His lips twitched, and he folded his arms across his chest. "So I've been told."

"I hate you."

He brushed a kiss across my forehead. An unwelcome heat spiraled through my body and my heart squeezed. My reaction didn't make sense, so I mentally chalked it up to the trauma of the last few weeks—starting with catching Evan cheating, and ending with my abduction.

"No, you don't," he drawled as he rose from the bed.

"I don't want to see you again. Can't someone else take care of me?"

He raised one eyebrow, a quick up and down motion that made me uneasy. "Who? Caesar?"

"Caesar? Who's he?"

"The man who tried to squeeze the life out of your neck a few seconds ago. Or maybe you'd prefer my father. I have a hunch you wouldn't like him very much either...he has a notoriously bad temper. Do want some tea or broth?"

*What the hell?* I blinked. "What?"

"Your throat is probably sore from Caesar's

70

attentions. Tea or broth might be better than solid food."

"I'll have tea with some whiskey."

He shook his head. "Sorry. It's not on the menu. Alcohol could make you more volatile, and it's not good for you anyway."

"Lots of things aren't good for me…like being locked in a cell, the lack of sunlight, being molested, but you don't seem to care about any of those things."

He scoffed. "You haven't been molested. Far from it."

Heat poured into my face as memories of the night in the bar with him flashed through my mind, taunting me with my stupidity. I turned to the side hoping he wouldn't notice.

"Are you blushing?"

"Hardly." I rolled my eyes. "Thanks to your buddy, Caesar, I don't feel well."

"If you say so," he replied. "Have a good night." He opened the door.

"What about the tea or the broth?" I reminded him, my voice panicked. Even though I didn't like him, I didn't want to be alone. I'd go crazy staring at the walls for hours without anything to do.

"I'll see what I can do."

He slammed the door behind him without glancing back.

"Dammit," I screamed, and the vibration raked like fire over my sore throat. I threw my pillow at the door. Tears flooded my eyes, clouding my vision. I was sick of crying and being sad. Fate had screwed with my life, and I didn't know if anything would feel right or safe again.

# Chapter Ten

Life rolled on and without a window or a clock, I didn't even know how many days had passed. A week was my best guess, but then again, I stopped counting after three days of confinement.

A man who never talked or made eye contact brought me three meals and escorted me on three bathroom breaks every day. When I asked him questions, he stared right through me. I even tried communicating in my rusty Spanish. My attempt didn't make a difference. Apparently, someone—most likely Ryker—told him not to talk to me. He delivered some books a couple days ago. They weren't something I'd normally read, but it was better than staring at the walls.

I craved conversation and contact. Yesterday, I started singing songs at the top of my lungs—dumb songs designed to annoy everyone in hearing distance. First, I belted out cornball nursery rhymes like the "Wheels on the Bus" and the "Ants Go Marching." I liked these two songs because they allowed me to invent new verses to the tune. When

I found myself talking about the drunks on the bus, I figured I should move on.

Move on I did…with Eric Carmen's "All by Myself" and Katy Perry's "Roar." Both songs appealed to me given my situation. One spoke to my loneliness, and the other became a theme song about breaking out my prison. I didn't know all the lyrics, but I improvised where necessary. As a bonus, I liked the idea of subjecting Ryker to my ramblings, because I had a feeling they would annoy the shit out of him.

"Get dressed," Ryker demanded one morning after I finished eating my breakfast.

I scanned my outfit. I had on the same dress I wore yesterday, not that my clothing selections were important. I didn't have anyone to impress. "I am dressed."

With narrowed eyes and a furrowed brow, he scanned the length of my body. "You wore that dress yesterday."

"How would you know?" I didn't look up from my book.

"Cameras."

Time froze as my mind swam in circles. "Cameras?" Somehow I found my voice, but it was small, barely above a whisper.

"Yes, cameras." He tilted his head to the side, a faint smile playing at the corners of his lush lips. "You know what those are, right?"

I wanted to say something cutting, but anger and shock prevented me from forming the words. While I was locked in a cave-like room, Ryker apparently scrutinized my movements as though I were a rat in a lab experiment. How long before Hattie lost her mind? "You're a sick bastard."

"I've heard that before. Let's go."

"Where are we going?"

"We're making a proof of life video, or in this case, a proof of life live video conference."

"That's dumb," I declared standing up.

"How do you figure?"

"I'm sure there's a way to trace the call and then they'll come for me. What are you using? Skype?"

He chuckled. "It's not Skype, just something similar with many layers of encryption."

"That doesn't mean they can't circumvent it."

"They could, but it will take at least seven minutes to break the encryption technology if they're good. Longer if they don't know what they're doing, and the exchange won't last long anyway." He held out his hand to me.

"So it's a live stream." Ignoring his hand, I brushed by him. I probably had about thirty seconds of saying whatever I wanted before they stopped me or turned off the video stream. I intended to make good use of the time even if Ryker and his minions punished me later. Given my solitary confinement in a windowless room, I didn't have much information to provide, but I refused to read from some worthless script where I begged my dad to comply with my captors' terms.

"You think you'll be able to give them useful information," he said. A ghost-like laugh escaped his mouth as he wrapped his hand around my neck, guiding me out the door.

Screw him. He was always one step ahead of me,

but that knowledge only fueled the fire raging inside of me to find a way to circumvent him. "Maybe," I replied.

He guided me through the shadowed hallways of the house that served as my prison for the past week. When we reached the front door, he pulled a rope from the pocket of his black pants and dangled it in front of my face. "Do I need this or will you be a good girl?"

My body begged with me to resist everything he wanted and try to escape, but with him trailing beside me, I wouldn't get far. In the end, he'd catch me, and he'd make my life much worse than it already was. If I did this chat, maybe it would improve my dad's chances of finding me or securing my release in the near future. I held out my hands to him. "Do whatever you want. With or without the restraints, I can't go far."

"You're right. I'll find you." He stuffed the rope back in his pocket and opened the door. "Now walk."

The minute I stepped outside the front door, my eyes screamed from the sudden onslaught of bright light. I'd spent over a week in a dark, cavernous room, and my eyes didn't appreciate the sudden change. Ryker's hand circled the back of my neck again.

"We're going to the villa to do the little video chat."

I nodded as my vision came into focus. Less than fifty yards in front of me, I saw a large, white stucco villa with sweeping arches and a terra cotta colored tile roof. It had to be at least three stories with a picturesque columned front patio. I glanced over my shoulder to see the building where Ryker kept me. Like the villa, it was white stucco, but it didn't have any windows—at least on the front of the building—and resembled a shed in comparison to the villa.

"What am I supposed to say to my dad?" I asked as Ryker pushed open an oversized, intricately carved wooden door.

"I don't think we'll be talking to your dad today."

I halted, and Ryker's body brushed against my back. Every inch of his heated body pressed into my back. I trembled. "Why not?"

His hand dropped from my neck and swept around my waist. "Your dad isn't our main point of contact."

I closed my eyes, trying to ignore the way his spicy scent wrapped around me, infiltrating my lungs, making me dizzy. "Then why are we bothering? I can't imagine many other people have a sufficient interest in securing my release in exchange for your brother."

"Senator Deveron," he breathed next to my neck. "Does his name ring any bells?"

"What?" I seethed through clenched teeth. "Why would he care?"

"You tell me."

"I don't know. You're the man with the answers."

He whirled me around to face him, his thumb stroking the soft, still bruised skin of my throat. I swallowed hard. As usual, his touch unnerved me, and I tensed my muscles so I didn't melt into him.

"He and his son are very interested in your safe return. In fact, their level of interest makes me question your little breakup story."

I shrugged, feigning indifference even as my heart raced at the thought of seeing Evan's face in a few minutes. Mixed…was the only word applicable to my jumbled emotions. Relieved he cared, angry he came to my rescue when my dad didn't or couldn't, and embarrassed I had sex with the man who kidnapped me. I hoped Evan didn't know that dirty fact because I intended to take it to my grave. "Why do you care whether we broke up or not?"

A wry smile lit the sharp angles of his face. "I don't care either way, but I need accurate information in order to fully understand the situation and react accordingly."

I turned my head to the side, unable to look at his face for one more second. "Right, I'm just part of your job…another chess piece to move and manipulate as needed to achieve the desired outcome."

"You're wrong." His fingers cradled my face, turning my chin so I had to look into his stormy gray eyes again.

"Wrong about what?" I whispered the words almost to myself.

"Do you really want to know?"

"Yes," I said even as I shook my head.

"Even if I met you at a different time in a different place, I would have pulled you out of that bar and fucked you against the wall, except it wouldn't have ended there," he drawled.

"It wouldn't have?" I said, mesmerized by his deep voice.

He shook his head. "I would have brought you back to my hotel and caressed every inch of your skin with my hands and my mouth until I burned you into my mind, and you had enough orgasms to last a lifetime. And then, I would have woke you up a few hours later to start all over again."

*Holy shit.* My knees felt weak, and I swayed into him as my body warred with my mind to collect on his promise.

"Breathe, Hattie. Breathe," he said.

I sucked in a deep breath. "You really want that? With me?" I whispered, the words barely audible.

He trailed a finger down my neck along my collarbone to the top of my breast. A fevered tremor tore through my body. "Of course," he answered without hesitating.

"Then, why don't you do it?" Even as the words tumbled from my lips, my mind pleaded with me to take them back. I couldn't be with him again. Ever. It was sick, twisted, and depraved I had even considered it. I should slap him across the face, but I didn't.

"I can't. Your life is waiting for you, and when you're safely ensconced in your bed with Evan in a week or two, you don't need to have any more regrets weighing you down."

"Why don't you let me decide what regrets I'm willing to live with?" I needed to sew my mouth shut.

A devastating grin had slid across his face before he laughed. His eyes crinkled at the corners, and a faint dimple made an appearance on the right side of his face. For a split second, I forgot to be offended, but then the sensual haze cleared.

"Don't patronize me." Jesus, what was wrong with me? My mind and body battled over him even as he laughed at the expense of my sanity.

He disguised his mouth with a quick swipe of his hand. "I'm not. Believe me, I like your enthusiasm, but it's better if I don't touch you again. In a couple months, I'll be a distant memory, and you won't even remember the color of my eyes."

"Maybe," I prevaricated as I shook my head. Whether or not this was the last instant I ever touched him or saw his face, I'd never forget him. I wished it weren't true. Trust me, the thought of five or ten years elapsing and still having wandering thoughts of Ryker—his sensual lips, his sexy grin, and the feel of his warm body pressed against mine—struck an apoplectic fear deep in my already wounded heart.

He dropped his hand from my body, I whimpered from the loss. "It's time to do the proof of life live feed."

"Do I have to read a script for them?"

"No. Just answer their questions. Nothing you say will change the outcome," he said mildly. He opened the double door in front of us and held out his hand. "After you."

# Chapter Eleven

I froze mid-step as I entered the room. The only two faces I'd seen since becoming a prisoner were in the room, plus another older man, flanked by two overweight men with machine guns draped over their shoulders.

"Hattie," Ryker said, resting the palm of his hand on my back. "You've met Caesar, and Javier."

So, Javier was the man who had brought me food and escorted me to the bathroom the past week. "Not officially," I mumbled folding my arms across my chest, glaring daggers at Caesar.

If Ryker heard me, he didn't bother acknowledging the comment. "And this," Ryker pointed to the man sitting behind the desk with graying hair, "is Ignacio Vargas."

The hairs on the back of my neck stood on end when my eyes met his. His eyes were black, blank, and devoid of any emotion except maybe hate, but maybe not even that. Looking at him was like staring into the abyss. Ignacio was Ryker's dad and the head of the Vargas Cartel. As much as I would've liked to ignore their connection, meeting him deprived me of the option. Ice crystals formed in my blood. *This is what it's like to look into the eyes of a killer*, my mind whispered.

"It's a pleasure to finally meet you," Ignacio said in perfect but heavily accented English. "I'm sorry we couldn't chat earlier, but I had other business monopolizing my attention." Standing up, he turned his attention to Ryker. "We should get started. Senator Deveron is waiting for our call."

"We need to discuss how this is going to work," Ryker declared.

Ignacio cut him off with an abrupt wave of his hand. "Miss Covington is going to answer a few questions. That's it, and I'm short on time today. We need to expedite this."

"Of course," Ryker replied as he slipped into the chair at the desk. His hands flew over the computer keyboard for a few minutes. Then, he stood up again and motioned to the chair. "Hattie, take a seat."

I didn't want to see Evan or his dad. I was afraid they would know what I did with Ryker...what I still wanted to do with him. It took all of my self-control not to flee from the room and run as fast and hard as my legs could carry me out of the villa and on the road to freedom. I retreated, taking a few anemic steps back, and one of Ignacio's guards lifted his gun. Shit. I wouldn't even make it out the door, much less out of the villa. I buried my shaking hands in the folds of my dress and settled into the chair.

Ryker squeezed my shoulder, then relocated to a

chair across the room. Ignacio quickly took his place behind me.

"Senator Deveron," Ignacio said as his image filled the computer screen in front of us. "Miss Covington is alive and well as you can see." He rested his hands on my shoulders and my breath accelerated to an uncomfortable level. I didn't want his hands on me. My skin crawled under his fingers, repulsion radiating from every pore.

"We'd like to ask her a few questions to ascertain her well-being." Senator Deveron adjusted his monitor, allowing me to see Evan and him. Evan looked pale and exhausted. Dark circles shadowed the skin around his eyes, and heavy stubble coated his normally clean-shaven face.

"Go ahead," Ignacio's hands dropped from my shoulders, and I took a deep breath trying to erase his touch from my mind and remain calm.

"Hattie," Evan breathed, inclining forward until his elbows rested on the table in front of him. "Are you okay?"

Seriously. How did he expect me to answer his question? Of course I'm not okay. I'm as far from okay as I could conceivably get. I'm being held captive by a ruthless cartel. "I'm alive," I said instead, dropping my eyes to my hands as they twisted the fabric of my dress. I was pretty sure my fingers would poke holes in the gauzy material by the end of the conversation.

"Are you hurt?" Evan persisted.

"Physically? No." I hedged, unable to answer that question either.

Evan stretched forward even further, his face

only inches from the screen, bringing the different colors in his eyes into sharp focus...black, gold, chocolate mixed with green flecks. "Nobody has *touched* you, right?"

My eyes flickered to Ryker. His face didn't give anything away. I thought I'd see a hint of what he wanted me to say, but his face didn't offer a single breadcrumb of information. Just before I returned my attention back to the computer monitor, his lips turned up at the corners, and his eyes flashed with a storm of lust, or maybe it was a trick of the light. Either way, that suggestive, fleeting glimpse of his thoughts transported my mind to an illicit daydream. It felt as though I had viewed a movie of us having sex against the wall on fast-forward. My heart stumbled inside my chest. What the hell was happening to me?

Volcanic heat rushed up my neck, and I tucked my head against my chest. "I want to go home," I whispered, ignoring the question entirely. "I really need to go home, Evan."

"As you can see, Hattie is alive and in good condition. When can I expect the exchange to happen?" Ignacio barked. Obviously his patience with Evan's questions had expired. I didn't care. Mine had too. As much as I wished otherwise, I didn't have any information to help them rescue me. I suspected I was still in Mexico, but I wasn't 100 percent certain, and Mexico was a huge country.

"We're working on it. Things like this don't happen overnight. Hattie's father is pursuing it from his angle, and I'm doing everything in my power to facilitate the prisoner exchange." Senator Deveron cleared his throat and reclined in his chair.

"I'm running out of patience. This needs to happen within the next week," Ignacio persisted, shifting impatiently from foot to foot.

"No way." Evan vaulted out of his chair. "That's impossible. We're not some third world banana republic with a dictator who can snap his fingers and make things magically happen."

"Figure it out." With those three words, Ignacio hooked his hand into the top of my hair, yanking it back, exposing my neck. His other hand curved around the front of my neck. Unfortunately, in that hand, he had a knife. He slid the knife across my neck up the side of my face. "I'd hate to have to hurt her or cause any permanent damage to this pretty face."

I squeezed my eyes closed, bracing myself for the moment his knife penetrated my skin. With each centimeter it slid along my skin, he pressed harder…deeper. I cataloged his movements.

Cheek.

Below my ear.

The underside of my jaw.

I wanted to scream, but my lungs constricted, preventing me from inhaling one molecule of air. I bit the inside of my bottom lip so hard the copper taste of blood flowed through my mouth. And then it happened…the sharp point of the knife bit into the side of my neck and a warm liquid trickled down my skin.

A piercing scream echoed through the room, and it took me a few seconds to realize it came from my mouth. Ice ripped through my muscles and my heart froze in my chest. It took every ounce of control to suck in another breath.

"What the fuck! You promised not to hurt her," Evan screamed, his voice cracking, but I didn't open my eyes. I didn't need to see his stricken face. I already had a shitstorm of emotions racing through my mind without adding his fear to mine. I was going to die…maybe not today, but soon. The Vargas Cartel had no intention of letting me live.

"I think you understand how serious this is now. Maybe you'll figure out how to make the wheels of justice churn a little faster," Ignacio warned. His voice vibrated through my body, as he withdrew the knife and stepped back.

"That's enough," Ryker said. I smelled his spicy, sea salt scent as he leaned over and shut off the computer monitor. The noise from the video conference halted mid-shouts. "We're done here. Everyone needs to leave."

Distantly, I heard the shuffle of feet as they exited the room, but I still refused to open my eyes. My brain was fuzzy with fragmented thoughts and racing fears. I wanted to go to sleep and wake up when I had my life back, and if that never happened, I didn't want to wake up at all.

When the heavy door slammed, I slumped down in the chair and opened my eyes. Everything was out of focus, coated with a dreamlike haze. Nothing seemed real. I couldn't comprehend how my vacation to Mexico had ended with me as a hostage.

Ryker crouched in front of me. "How do you feel?"

Not able to talk, I meekly shook my head.

He lifted my hand and held two fingers on the inside of my wrist, checking my pulse. "Shit," he murmured. "You need to lie down."

In one swift movement, he lifted me out of the chair, cradling me against his body. Like human chains, I wrapped my arms around his neck as though he was my one and only lifeline, and everything would fall apart if I let go.

# Chapter Twelve

One.

Two.

Three.

Four turns and Ryker halted in front of a door at the end of the hallway in the villa. He pushed it open and kicked it closed behind us. Maneuvering through the large room, he carried me with ease. Instead of white walls and dull concrete floors like my prison cell, the room danced with vibrant color—warm terra cotta floor tiles, honeyed wood furniture, a black and red Aztec looking coverlet neatly folded at the bottom of a creamy duvet. Bright photographs of Mayan villages hung in a block of nine on the heavily textured wall above the headboard. A lamp molded from a twisted wooden branch casted a yellow glow over the room.

He sat me down on the bed, and my eyes drifted lazily over the room absorbing the details. "Where are we?"

"My room."

I shivered. "Why?"

He didn't answer. "Get under the covers and warm up."

I glanced at my hands. Blood stained my fingertips. My eyes widened, and I thought I'd be sick. On a good day, the sight of blood made me lightheaded, but today it was so much worse. I didn't have my usual armor. I'd been stripped bare by the events of the past week and the past hour. "Oh my God," I breathed as I leaned against the mountain of pillows on his bed.

Ryker sat next to me on the bed. "Are you going to be sick?" he asked slowly.

I closed my eyes and took deep breaths. "No," I whispered, not opening my eyes. "I don't like blood."

"Shh," he said, taking the hem of my dress and lifting it.

"Get away from me," I yelled, swatting my hands at him like a loose helicopter rotor system. Whatever calm I felt in his arms melted when I saw my blood. Ignacio Vargas, Ryker's dad, had sliced my neck. I gasped for breath repeatedly, but my lungs forcibly repelled the air. It was like someone had stuffed a ball of plastic wrap in my mouth, slowly but inexorably suffocating me.

"Calm down," he said, restraining my arms.

"Calm down!" I screamed. "How am I supposed to calm down? I'm being held captive by a band of deranged murderers, one of which sliced open my neck and threatened to kill me." He snorted, and my eyes popped open. Summoning every inch of fiery anger from every corner of my soul, I glared at him.

"Nobody is going to kill you."

"Don't lie to me."

"I'm not lying. Ignacio is first and foremost a businessman. He'd sell you into the sex trade before he'd kill you."

My mouth hung open, and my hands dropped onto the mattress like limp noodles. "I'd rather die." I had read the stories. Being sold into the sex trade was a death sentence, albeit a long, torturous one where I'd become a shell of myself before I took my final breath.

"Good thing you won't have to make that choice in the near future." Without an explanation, he picked me up again and carried me to the bathroom adjoining his room. My sandals fell off my feet as he dumped me in the shower, still fully dressed.

Cold, then hot water beat against my skin. Joining me in the partially enclosed shower, he stripped my soaked dress over my head and scrubbed every inch of my skin. I stood there, unmoving and trembling from his touch and the tsunami of emotions assaulting my brain. His hands moved in efficient, asexual strokes, coating every inch of my skin in a thin veil of white foam. Then, he moved me under the spray of hot water again.

With tightly closed eyes, I tipped my head to the ceiling wishing I could follow the water down the drain and get the hell out of this place. "I want to go home. I want my life back. Is that too much to ask?" I whispered, more to myself than Ryker.

"No." He turned off the water and wrapped a big, white terry cloth robe around my body, directing my arms into the oversized sleeves.

Again, he lifted me and placed me on the edge of

the countertop. Using a white washcloth, he gently cleaned the laceration on my neck. "It's not too deep," he whispered, his face only inches from neck. His warm breath licked the side of my face, making me too aware of his proximity. "It won't leave a scar."

I scanned every feature of his face, studying him as though he were a single cell organism under a microscope. Searching for what? A flaw? Kindness? Redemption? I didn't know. I didn't find any clues or secrets hidden in the details of his flawlessly sculpted face. He had one of those faces where if I separated any feature from the whole, it wouldn't be perfect, but together they were a study in rugged, masculine perfection.

Water marred his starched white linen shirt making it transparent, hinting at the muscles my hands freely explored over a week ago. His almost black hair brushed the collar of his shirt. The sleeves of his shirt were rolled to his elbow, exposing his golden and thickly muscled forearms. As usual, dark stubble highlighted the chiseled angles of his face, and my mind taunted me with the memory of it abrading my neck as he devoured me. And in that stretch of time, with Ryker tending to my injury, I felt like a rare rose blossoming under his attention. My lips twitched at the silly analogy.

He slipped a long elegant finger underneath my chin. "What are you thinking?"

I blinked repeatedly as though the motion would somehow scrub away the dangerous direction of my thoughts. "How I'd kill for a spa day," I lied. But what was one more lie between abductor and abductee? He didn't need to know my mind was freefalling into Stockholm syndrome.

"When in doubt, choose the massage over the facial." He didn't make eye contact as he smeared an ointment on my cut. I flinched, and his gray eyes snapped to mine.

"Does your girlfriend agree with you?" What was wrong with me? Did I really go *there*? Yes, I went *there*. I mentally bitch slapped myself. I didn't care if he had a girlfriend. I didn't care if he had a whole harem chained in the dungeon of this villa or wherever he spent the bulk of his time.

Ryker's hands stilled, and he lifted one dark eyebrow, a hundred questions dangling from the tip of his tongue. "My girlfriend?" he said dryly as he smoothed a few butterfly bandages on my neck.

"Yes. You know what one of those are, don't you?"

"Hm." He trailed his finger along my neck, to my collarbone. His eyes flickered to mine as he slid the top of my robe down my shoulder. Goosebumps scattered across my skin, but I didn't budge. I didn't take a single breath. I couldn't.

"What are you doing?" My voice was strangled.

His eyes never leaving mine, he ran two fingers down my exposed shoulder and along the side of my breast. "Touching you," he admitted, his voice soft, his hands drawing circles on my needy skin.

I liked it. It made me feel alive as I teetered on the cliff of madness. I closed my eyes and bit my lip to stifle any sound that might betray my thoughts. I pictured his touch like a flame and myself like a piece of paper reduced to ashes under the pads of his very capable fingers. Not good. I searched my mind for any remnants of hatred or repulsion, but his touch must have turned those emotions to ash too.

His breath hovered near the tip of my breast and...what the fuck? My nipples pebbled. If he touched me, I'd explode. Air escaped my mouth in uneven, jagged pants, and I didn't know whether it was from arousal, fear, self-loathing, or just an all-around mind fuck.

Then, he did it. He captured the tip of my nipple with his mouth as he shoved the robe off my other shoulder. I expelled a long, guttural breath and my back arched of its own volition. I was like a stupid zebra offering my heart to the lion for a Sunday afternoon snack by the water hole. I blamed my reaction on temporary insanity brought on by extreme stress.

"Do you like this?" he asked as his mouth shifted to my other nipple and drew the peak into his mouth with a hard suck. And reminiscent of the last time he touched me, both pleasure and pain swirled together creating something bigger...better. "Do you want me to continue?"

My brain scrambled to process his question, but it came up empty. I should've been focused on a plan of escape, but Ryker's attentions didn't leave room for plotting. Instead, I concentrated on the heat of his mouth, branding my sensitive flesh, speculating what his mouth would feel like pressed on other parts of my body.

He parted my thighs and positioned himself between them. I should've pushed him away, but I spread them further, rolling out the welcome mat. Come and get me. I'm so stupid.

His hand slid from my breast all the way down my stomach, hovering, teasing, and waiting for I didn't know what. Then, I remembered I never answered his question, and I wouldn't. I'd never give voice to my lust for him. Never.

One of my hands found his shoulder and the other circled his wrist, sliding it lower. He resisted, and I felt like dying. And then his eyes caught mine, holding me hostage. "Answer," he murmured, his finger dipping less than an inch lower.

I shook my head. "I can't say it." My eyes pleaded with him, locking us in a silent tug of war. Eyes flashed. Lips curled. No other words were exchanged. He refused to give me what I wanted, and I refused to give him what he wanted. I would have rather burned up in flames than surrendered the last sliver of my dignity to him.

Just when I convinced myself he'd leave me unfulfilled, he dropped to his knees, and I whimpered realizing exactly what he planned to do. His tongue grazed the length of my slick entrance and a surge of forbidden electricity ripped through my body. "Oh," I moaned as my head fell forward. At that instant, my body welcomed the diversion he promised in his wicked gaze.

He licked, nibbled, and everything between until I became a boneless, moaning version of myself I didn't recognize. I pressed my eyes closed, so I didn't have a visual to go with my body's betrayal of my soul. I couldn't explain why I let him—no, begged him to do this—but the words or desire to stop him evaded me, shimmering so far out of reach I had no choice but to surrender.

Lost in the moment, I lifted my hips to encourage him. I started to slip off the counter, but his hands dug into my hips, shoving me back until my back hit the mirror. His finger circled my sex, and I clenched so tight the sugary bliss of pleasure spiraled through me, but it didn't compare to the second when he closed his mouth over me again, stealing my very essence. My body no longer belonged to me.

Tremors cascaded down my spine, and any last ounce of willpower I possessed splintered into a million pieces. Desperate, I buried my hands in his hair, squirming toward him, making sure he didn't renege on the promises he made with every indecent stroke of his tongue and flick of his skilled fingers.

Blood pounded through my head, and I forgot everything but the wildfire raging inside of me. Then, out of nowhere, he slid two fingers inside of me, and I came apart. My body shook with spasms of pleasure so deep that I felt it in my bones. Every time I thought it was over, another tremor rocked through me until I was utterly exhausted.

And there it was…another orgasm courtesy of Ryker, my captor. My enemy. My tormentor. It didn't take more than a few seconds for the guilt and self-loathing to swallow me. Unbidden, tears erupted from my eyes, and emotionally, I was right back where I started after Ignacio cut me; except now, everything was worse. Much worse.

I inhaled, trying to pull giant mouthfuls of air into my lungs, but it felt as though a vise grip was slowly, inexorably tightening around my chest with every passing tick of the clock.

"Nice work," I snarled, shoving him away from me with wild, shaky hands. I stuffed my arms through the discarded robe, squeezing it closed at the base of my neck as though it were a bulletproof vest, sheltering the last pieces of my dignity from his eyes.

He wiped the tears from my face with the palm of his hand, and at any other time, with any other guy, I might have believed the gesture was thoughtful...romantic even. The little I knew of Ryker told me there was a far simpler answer. Most likely, he didn't appreciate the inconvenience of my tears.

"Work?" he questioned, his voice deceptively soft, his gray eyes mesmerizing.

"Yeah, like the night at the bar you used sex to distract me." My body trembled from the overwhelming emotions poisoning my mind and body.

"Did it work?"

With those words, he destroyed me. Silence would have been better than that. My flash of angry rebellion melted into pathetic sobs. I dropped my head to my chest, and my arms circled my body, trying to hold the shattered pieces of my soul together. I'd rather he sliced me with a knife over and over than use sexual warfare as his weapon of choice. "I think I'm going to be sick."

Without hesitation, he wrapped his arms around me, comforting me, and I let him. Slowly, he rocked me back and forth for I didn't know how many agonizing seconds, then carried me once again to his bed.

The minute my body touched the mattress, I curled into a ball, a limp effigy of my former self. I closed my eyes, shutting out the world around me and welcoming the darkness whispering my name.

The mattress dipped under Ryker's weight as he stretched out beside me. I braced for his touch, but it never happened. Gratitude and disappointment collided inside of my heart, confusing me even more. I funneled my anger toward him, tossing silent accusations in his direction from the safety of my cocooned mind and shuttered eyes. And yet, he didn't notice. Like a seductive menace, he lazed next to me, unmoved and uncaring, his very presence stealing my air and safety.

"Sleep," he said after few minutes, his voice hypnotic in its intensity, musical in its beauty. "You need to rest."

Minutes stretched into an hour or more as I drifted in the world somewhere between sleep and wakefulness, neither state fully claiming me, because I was too busy drowning in the murky waters of regret and self-loathing. A life preserver couldn't save me at this point. I'd need a coast guard fleet.

Then, it started.

Feather soft touches along my face.

Whispered fingertips along my arms.

A soft humming.

And, like magic, oblivion claimed me.

# Chapter Thirteen

A draft of cool air roamed over my skin when the blanket lifted from my body. Instantly alert, I cracked one eyelid. Moonlight filtered into the room, casting eerie shadows on the stucco walls.

Ryker lifted his shirt over his head and dropped it on the floor, revealing smooth, golden skin. Funny, I had sex with Ryker, but I never saw him naked. I didn't even know if he had hair on his chest. He didn't. He had a faint line of hair starting beneath his navel and disappearing under the waistband of his swim trunks. Apparently, he planned to go swimming and leave me in his room.

I closed my eyes again, partly because I didn't want him to realize I was awake, and partly because I wanted to shut him out of my mind and my life. His feet shuffled over the floor, and then I finally heard the sound I was waiting for…the click of the door. I was alone in his bedroom.

I stalled for several long minutes to see if he'd return. The deafening silence of the room and villa echoed unnaturally in my ears. In fact, I could almost hear the tropical wind as it caressed the trees outside the window. Cautiously, I sat up, taking in the luxurious surroundings. I hardly noticed them when Ryker carried me here hours ago, but their warmth seemed strangely out of place given what little I knew of the Vargas Cartel. For some reason, I thought the decorations should reflect the ruthless nature of its inhabitants.

I ran my hand over the cut on my neck. It still throbbed, but less than when it happened. And that was a blessing, because I intended to seize my moment of freedom and disappear into the night.

Tightening my robe around my waist, I walked to the bathroom in search of my shoes and my dress. I scooped up the wet, shredded dress from the tile floor, and I slipped on my sandals. I shuddered envisioning roaming the wilderness wearing it. I'd prefer being stark naked. I ripped a strip of material from the hem, balled up the dress, and tossed it in the direction of the trashcan under the floating travertine countertop.

Using the torn fabric, I crafted a headband to keep my hair out of my eyes. Normally, I liked the way my long bangs framed my face, but I needed to see every detail if I planned to outthink and outrun Ryker and his band of merry murderers.

Stalking back into the bedroom, I flung open Ryker's dresser drawer, tossing clothes on the floor until I found something suitable to wear. I slipped on a plain, black t-shirt and a pair of gym shorts with a drawstring. As much as I hated to take anything linking me to him, I'd wear Ryker's clothes if it meant I'd have a chance to escape. And that faint spicy, sea salt scent lingering on his clothes could go fuck itself.

Once I had clothes to wear, I searched the entire contents of his dresser looking for a weapon. Not finding anything in his dresser, I moved to his nightstand. Except for a lone Bible, the nightstand was empty. The irony of finding a Bible in his nightstand didn't escape me.

Maybe Ryker spent his nights confessing his lengthy list of sins as he recited verses of forgiveness. Momentarily defeated, I sat down on the bed. I needed something useful. My mind rattled through the options: a knife, a bat, a metal closet rod—and then I remembered my dad kept a gun tucked in the side rails of his bed frame.

Sliding to the floor on all fours, I ran my hand along the side of the mattress. Bingo. Cautiously, I pulled the gun from its hiding place. A Glock 26. I pumped my free arm in the air. Thank you, Dad, for making me take a gun safety course before I went to college.

Clenching the gun in one hand, I pointed the barrel toward the corner, making sure to keep my finger away from the trigger guard. I didn't need to shoot myself in the foot. Ryker would probably let me bleed to death. I pressed the magazine release button and pulled out the magazine. *Yes.* It was my lucky day. The gun was loaded. I slid the magazine back into the gun and stood up. Showtime.

With as little noise as possible, I turned the doorknob, and inch-by-painfully-slow-inch I cracked the door open. When I didn't hear anything, I slipped out the door with my back pressed to the wall.

The plaster walls were humid and sticky, sweating against my skin and clothes as I slunk through the hallway. My ears strained, processing and interpreting every creak, shift, and murmur in the otherwise unnaturally silent villa.

Then, I heard hushed voices. At least two men hovered near the end of the hallway, speaking Spanish. Not for the first time, I cursed myself for not continuing with my Spanish classes after high school. I closed my eyes concentrating on the words, but they blurred together. I heard Senator Deveron's name and the word *hijo*, which meant son. Other than that, I couldn't decipher anything.

I tried to keep my breathing slow and quiet, but my heart had a mind of its own. It thudded wildly in my chest, and my mind flew through my options. None of them were good. I could sneak back into Ryker's room and let fate take its course, or I could wait until the men relocated to another room...or found me. Ryker's words about Ignacio being a businessman first and selling me into the sex trade floated through my mind, and I shivered. Fuck no. I couldn't stay here. I had a chance to escape, and I needed to seize it with both hands.

Pointing the gun toward the end of the hall, I remained flush against the wall. Sweat coated my hairline, and my entire body shook so hard, I had to support the gun with both hands to keep it steady. Time crawled, and just when I thought my heart fully intended to burst in my chest, the voices faded then disappeared entirely. My feet whispered down the corridor, simulating a delicate ballet prance.

One step.

Two more steps.

Five steps.

I counted every step, feeding off the power and control each one offered.

When I reached the end of the hall, I peeked around the corner. Empty. Thank God. Finally, some luck had flipped in my favor. I didn't hesitate for one more second. Leading with my gun, I tiptoed into the vaulted living room.

My eyes skated over the large, overstuffed white sofa, the rattan chairs, and finally, the long wall of glass doors at the back of the room. There it was…freedom, dangling less than fifty feet in front of me. I could do this. I could really escape.

The thought injected adrenaline into my previously sluggish veins. I ran, hoping, praying, and pleading with every stride that the doors weren't connected to an alarm system—and if they were, that some overworked soul had forgotten to set it. My sandaled feet slapped against the tiled floor, echoing off the voluminous beamed ceiling.

My momentum nearly propelled me into the wall of glass, but at the last minute, my foot clipped a chair leg. I lost my footing and fell to my knees. My head snapped forward, and my teeth collided with the tip of my tongue. The distinct copper taste of blood flavored my mouth.

Shit.

Shit.

Shit.

Afraid to move, afraid to breathe, my eyes tracked the shadows through the room waiting for someone to find me. Long minutes had passed before I had enough courage to rise to my feet. This time I didn't rush it. I twisted the lock to the right as slow as possible to minimize the sound. When I heard a click, I expelled every last molecule of air from my lungs and pushed the door open.

I didn't wait for the alarm or any other sign of life from the villa. I ran, not even bothering to close the door behind me. Almost immediately, sultry jungle air wrapped around my skin like a wet blanket, strangling my chest and weighing down my steps.

Twigs snapped under my feet, the dense foliage scraped my skin, and rocks infiltrated the hard soles of my sandals. Without the benefit of any light from the villa, I could barely see five feet in front of me, but I didn't hesitate. For the first time in over a week, I was free, and I refused to stop running until I'd put a couple miles between the villa and me.

At home, I jogged eight- to ten-minute miles every other day, but that was in a park with paved pathways and relatively linear routes. Given the rough terrain, I needed to run at least thirty minutes before I slowed to a walk. That might give me the lead I needed to find a town or someplace with a phone.

What seemed like an eternity of cuts, scrapes, and one nearly twisted ankle later, my body rebelled, refusing to continue for one more second. With my lungs burning and my chest heaving, I stopped, bending at the waist, cursing my need for water. My throat was so dry I could hardly swallow.

*Stupid.*

*Fucking stupid.*

*Beyond fucking stupid.*

Disbelief ricocheted through me. I hadn't bothered with any supplies except a gun. I couldn't exactly drink the bullets. Silently, I cursed my dad for not forcing me to take a wilderness survival course in addition to the gun safety class. With my limited knowledge of the area, I'd be lucky if I ever found a road, much less one that led to somewhere other than the depths of this godforsaken jungle. Most likely, I'd wander further and further into the jungle until I collapsed dead from exhaustion, and whatever wildlife frequented this area would eventually pick my bones clean. I shuddered as I imagined rotting away in the jungle.

I rested on a nearby rock and surveyed my surroundings. What was that phrase my dad always used? Work smarter not harder. Yep, that was it. It was exactly what I needed to do. Now that I had put some distance between the villa and myself, I needed to open my eyes, take in my surrounding, and plan my escape.

Complaining wouldn't get me anywhere. My stomach rumbled, my mouth resembled cotton, my feet throbbed, and my eyelids weighed a thousand pounds. So what? I was free.

Squinting, I tried to scout a landmark or trail leading anywhere but back to the villa. I didn't see much of anything except dark shadows and more trees and underbrush. But then, I heard a noise. It sounded like the low hum of a convoy of trucks or other motorized vehicles.

My body froze. For a few beats, the frantic

pounding of my heart muffled whatever I thought I heard, but it didn't last long. The hum of vehicles turned into a muted roar, drowning out the sounds of the night and my thundering heart. I tried to convince myself my mind was playing a trick on me, but that didn't last longer than a few seconds. The faint glow of headlights in the distance lit up the inky black sky. I counted them.

One set.

Two sets.

Three sets.

Four sets.

Hunger, thirst, and tiredness forgotten, I sprinted in the opposite direction of the lights, eating up the terrain one giant stride at a time. I didn't know if the convoy had anything to do with the Vargas Cartel, but I immediately dismissed the idea of waiting around until I figured it out.

The ground was slippery beneath my feet. Branches whipped my face, probably leaving marks, but cuts and scratches healed, and they wouldn't kill me. On the other hand, the Vargas Cartel or any other criminal element roaming the jungle in the dead of the night might do exactly that. I suspected Ignacio's little slice along my neck would be tame in comparison to what would happen if they captured me again.

Not more than ten or so minutes later, I tripped over an exposed tree root, and I flew face first into the dirt. Every inch of my body ached, and bone-deep shooting pains radiated through my ankle. I wiggled it. Holy shit. I bit back a scream. It killed. I wasn't going anywhere tonight unless I crawled on all fours, and even then, I wouldn't get far. During the fall, tiny rocks had torn the skin of my knees and palms.

I rolled to my side and cradled my body against a tree trunk. Dirt and leaves coated my skin, and as I closed my eyes, I said a little prayer that it would be enough camouflage to conceal me for a while.

I needed to rest for a few minutes…

Maybe an hour.

# Chapter Fourteen

My eyes fluttered open briefly and then closed again. I was hot. No, hot didn't adequately describe it. I kicked off the damp sheet smothering my body and flipped onto my stomach, but the position didn't reduce my discomfort.

My body vibrated with pain. My stomach felt empty, and my eyes were dry and gritty. I groaned, rolling onto my back again, not opening my eyes.

"Are you in pain?"

I shot up in the bed, instantly awake. I scanned the room, but nothing looked familiar. Transparent netting hung from the ceiling, enclosing the bed in a haze of billowing white material. Bright light poured in through the open windows, and shadows of palm trees danced along the light yellow plaster walls. It looked like it was still morning, but I couldn't be sure.

And then I saw him. "Ryker?" The words came out strained and barely recognizable to my own ears.

He stood up from a dark brown wooden bench

beside the bed and pushed aside the netting. His eyes scrutinized every inch of my body. "You should sleep longer," he finally said.

I shook my head, trying to remember how I ended up here. I remembered falling in the jungle and deciding to rest. I suppose I fell asleep instead. "How?" My voice cracked.

"I found you."

I didn't respond. Instead, my mind circled repeatedly, chasing down my lost memories. I had a vague impression of being in the back seat of a jeep-like vehicle. The sky was just starting to transform from black to gray as my body rolled from side to side with each jarring bump, but beyond that…I didn't remember anything. I nodded. "Where am I?" The rudimentary furniture didn't resemble anything I'd seen in the villa, and the room had a window, so I wasn't in another windowless prison cell on the villa grounds.

He ignored my question and sat on the bed next to my hip. I scrambled away, but his hand came down hard on my thigh, stopping my retreat. Heat rushed through me, and goose bumps erupted on my leg despite my determination to remain unaffected by him. No. Not again.

His eyes dropped to my leg, and he smiled a lush, upward curve of his lips. My breath caught in my throat. His touch wasn't particularly predatory or sexual, but my body didn't get the message. Alert and standing at attention, my body wanted him even as my mind screamed a loud, resounding, *no fucking way*.

"Are you thirsty?"

I wanted to tell him no, but I was so thirsty and hungry I caved. I nodded. "And hungry."

A lazy grin floated across his lips, and my treasonous heart fluttered with mischief. "Good. Breakfast should arrive in a few minutes." His hand roamed down my leg to my knee and then my foot. Red lashes and purples bruises blanketed my legs from my knees to my feet. "You didn't answer my question. Are you in pain?"

"I'll live," I said, snatching my foot out of his hand. His touch scrambled my brain and turned my thoughts inside out. "Well, maybe not now that you found me," I amended with a shrug of one of my shoulders. "Are you going to kill me? Punish me?"

His eyebrows lifted, but he didn't respond because someone with less than perfect timing knocked on the door. I wanted to know what he planned to do to me.

"That's your breakfast." He stood up, but after few steps, he paused with his hand on the doorknob. "You can scream or say whatever you want when I open the door. It won't matter. This bed and breakfast is under the protection of the Vargas Cartel."

I scrambled out of the bed. "And what does that mean?"

"That they exist because we let them exist." My blank look didn't escape his notice. "The owners of the bed and breakfast pay the Vargas Cartel a monthly quota or tax to ensure their business isn't disturbed. The owners won't jeopardize the arrangement to save some random American girl."

"Like in the old movies about Al Capone where

109

businesses had to pay for protection from the mafia."

"Exactly. The Vargas Cartel taxes bars, discos, and hundreds of other small businesses." Ryker shrugged. "It makes the businesses complicit in the crime network and secures the cartel's territory."

I folded my arms across my chest, as my optimism of finding help dwindled with every word that left Ryker's mouth. "How did you explain showing up last night with an unconscious woman, or is that a normal occurrence for you?"

He glanced over his shoulder. "I told them you're my girlfriend."

"Asshole," I mumbled under my breath, but my insult didn't faze him. He chuckled as he opened the door.

"Ricardo. *Buenas tardes*," Ryker said when he opened the door. "*Gracias por complaciente mi novia y yo.*"

"*¡Por supuesto!*"

"Look, Hattie. He brought you food," Ryker said, glancing over his shoulder before he returned his attention to Ricardo. "*Gracias.*"

The man smiled at me, a wide welcoming smile, displaying a gold-capped front tooth. "*Su novio es hermosa.*"

"*Si, gracias.*"

Ryker pivoted to me again. "Say thank you to Ricardo."

"Why?"

"He said you're beautiful."

I folded my arms across my chest. "I guess he's into the dirty, unkempt look."

"You look fine. I cleaned you up last night."

I gawked at Ricardo. He had a huge smile on his face. He probably thought he'd earned a lifetime of favors by accommodating the son of the head of the Vargas Cartel and his girlfriend. "*Gracias*," I muttered, trying to smile, but I think it came out more like a grimace given the look on his face.

Ryker handed me the tray of food. "Will this work?"

"I prefer a lighter breakfast, but it will work." It was a lie. I'd eat my hand if I had to, but I hated accepting anything from him, even if I was desperate.

Ryker raised one eyebrow. "Lighter?" he questioned.

I shrugged. "I don't know. I usually eat yogurt with chia seeds and fresh fruit."

"I don't think they have that," he snapped before accompanying Ricardo out of the room, closing the door behind him.

The room didn't have a table, so I sat down on the bed and surveyed the food—eggs, toast, ham, and freshly squeezed orange juice. It would do just fine.

By the time Ryker returned, I had scraped my plate clean. As he sat next to me on the bed, I kept my eyes lowered, staring at my bare plate and empty glass like the answer to the universe would be found somewhere in the crumbs or film of orange liquid coating the bottom of my glass.

He held out a bottle of water. "Here," he said. "You're probably still thirsty."

I nodded my thanks but never met his eyes. My

unease vibrated through the room, taking on a life of its own. So many issues dangled in the air: my escape, my capture, my future, but most disconcerting was the fact that I practically begged him to touch me again. All of it hung around my neck like a noose waiting for the right moment to squeeze the life out of me.

As my mind raced, his cold, gray eyes never looked away. I squirmed under his knowing stare. I considered what he saw. I questioned what he was thinking. I wondered what he planned to do with me. I debated what happened to the gun I stole from his room. I couldn't take the silence any longer. "Why don't you have an accent?" I finally said, blurting out the first inane thought that entered my head.

"My mother is an American. I lived with her during the school year, and I lived with Ignacio during the summer."

"They weren't married?" I asked, fidgeting with my hands.

"No." He didn't elaborate.

"What about your brother? Where did he live?"

"With Ignacio and his wife. We don't have the same mother."

"Oh. Where does your mom live?"

"Connecticut now, but New York when I was younger."

"How did they meet?" I didn't have a clue why I wanted to ask these questions. Maybe I wanted to avoid heavier topics. Maybe I hated the charged silence, or maybe I wanted to know something about the man who repeatedly frayed my self-control and inspired my hate and lust in equal measure.

"At a photo shoot at a hotel owned by Dad's family. My mom was a model. He saw her, and the rest was history. She fell in love. He had a wife. He refused to leave her."

"Even when she got pregnant?" I shouldn't have continued the interrogation. It wasn't my business.

He paused, not answering for a prolonged second. "She gave him an ultimatum and he let her walk."

"Oh."

"Is that enough personal information for you?"

"Sorry." My eyes shot up. The minute my eyes met his, I was sorry I didn't have more control over my body. He held his stubborn jaw on an angle, and his faint smile parted his deceptively seductive mouth, exposing a hint of his white teeth. He was shockingly handsome, and the fact that I even noticed at a time when my life was dangling from a thread unsettled me more than I wanted to admit.

"Am I making you uncomfortable?"

"No," I said glaring at him, battling every disconcerting emotion with every last bit of willpower I had buried in the depths of my soul.

"Now, that's a lie if I've ever heard one." Before I had the opportunity to move, two of his surprisingly gentle fingertips brushed across my mouth, and I tensed, refusing to allow my body to respond. Despite my intentions, the heat of his touch spread like an inferno through my body, and I wanted to move away. I really did, but I didn't do a thing.

He bent his head toward mine until less than an inch remained between our foreheads. For some reason, the lingering distance was more lethal than if our skin actually made contact. Maybe it was the anticipation of his touch, or that his steely gray eyes were mesmerizing. I couldn't explain it, but his mere presence paralyzed me.

He slid the handmade headband from my hair, dropping it on the bed. "Better," he whispered, his eyes searching mine. "I like the way your hair frames your face."

I swallowed hard, trapped in the prison of his too watchful eyes.

"What are you afraid of? What do you think is going to happen right now?" His forehead finally brushed mine, and I held my breath.

*Do not breathe.*

*Do not breathe.*

*Ignore him.*

*Ignore his tantalizing scent.*

*Ignore his hypnotic eyes.*

*Ignore the sound of his voice.*

"Do you think I'm going to take advantage of you?"

His dark velvet voice meandered down my spine, and I tensed my muscles, hoping to fend off my reaction. "I wouldn't be surprised. You have a track record of doing exactly that." I tried to sound indifferent. I even accompanied my words with an exaggerated eye roll, but the words had a mind of their own. They came out wobbly and unconvincing.

"Are you sure about that?"

"Yes, and you know it. You take advantage of me whenever you sense even the faintest hint of vulnerability."

"Are you telling me you're vulnerable right now?"

I pressed the palm of my hand against his chest, trying to maintain even a small fragment of space. He was too close. Too overwhelming. Too imposing. Too heart-stopping. Too everything.

"Why are you doing this? You don't want me. This is about finishing the job...getting that precious pardon for your brother. You're just trying to..." I fisted the fabric of his shirt in hand, twisting it, madly searching for the magic words to combat him. "I don't know," I whispered.

"Trying to what? Kiss you? Kill you? Seduce you? Make you forget?" he said in his signature low, rugged voice that never failed to melt me from the inside out.

"All of the above. I don't know anymore. I'm confused. You confuse me. Whatever this is between us confuses me," I admitted. The minute the words fell out of my mouth, I groaned. But that didn't stop my body from drifting toward him like a magnet, unable to resist his lure. What was wrong with me?

A spine-tingling smile burst across his face, and I practically tasted my capitulation, both bitter and sweet as it coated my tongue. From the smirk on his face, he realized it too. Evidently, when it came to Ryker, I was Pavlov's dog responding every time he rang that fucking bell. No matter his tactics, no matter how much he annoyed me, no matter if he planned to kill me, I surrendered every time he summoned me.

"Stop fighting me. You know you don't want to."

He was a snake charmer. Didn't he realize I couldn't fight him? I shook my head, rejecting him, but he realized it was symbolic in nature, not an actual rejection. My eyes fluttered closed, embracing my defeat. He'd spun the web, and I was his willing victim, tangled in his silky prison.

The minute his lips grazed mine, my body came alive, and I fought back with the only weapon I had—my body. I became the aggressor. My mouth opened, searching, demanding, raiding, and he let me in. In an instant, his tongue slid against mine, and I sucked, bit, and took everything he offered and more, because he'd already stolen everything from me.

He gave just as good as he got, battling me with his mouth and hands, taking what he wanted and giving only what he wanted. He fought dirty, and within seconds, a hunger unlike anything I'd ever felt blazed through every cell in my body.

"I hate you," I said against his mouth, even as my hands pulled him closer. It was the truth. I hated that I failed to say no to him. I hated that he'd hijacked my life. But most of all, I hated that he made me feel more alive than Evan ever had. Even when our relationship was shiny and new, I'd never experienced the raw, white-knuckling desperation I felt with Ryker. For Ryker.

"I know," he responded, his eyes stormy and urgent like thunderstorms gathering on the edge of the horizon. He shoved me onto my back, and his body followed, hovering over me, watching me, challenging me, and I fought.

Wrapping my legs around his waist, I arched into him. "I wish I never met you." My hands slipped under the hem of his shirt, gliding over the chiseled peaks and valleys of his sculpted chest. As much as I wanted to touch him, I wanted to hurt him. I raked my nails down his chest, but he didn't flinch. He didn't even blink. *Fucker*.

"I know." His mouth moved to my neck and goose bumps scattered down my arms. Why did my body betray me time and time again with Ryker?

I rocked against him, one hand fisted in his hair, and the other yanked on the front of his shirt. I would rather spontaneously combust than ask him for anything, but my body literally ached for more contact, more of him. Mercifully, he understood me, moving against me with punishing force.

I didn't know how long we continued our twisted game...battling each other, manipulating each other. As hard as I pushed, he'd push back, not taking it any further than he wanted. Instead, we were like two hamsters going round and round...kissing, licking, touching, and grinding against each other, over and over, replay after replay, but nothing more.

Control.

Dominance.

Superiority.

You name it; we battled for it. Instead of using weapons, we used our mouths, our hands, our bodies, and our minds...until fire licked my hypersensitized flesh and every nerve ending prickled with both pleasure and pain.

Frustration mushroomed inside of me, bit by bit, second by second. A freefall of rioting and contradictory emotions crossed swords inside my mind. My ability to think logically failed, splintering like a paper-thin piece of wood. I was self-destructing under his assault.

Frantic to shift the pendulum in my direction, I tore at his belt buckle, my hands shaky from the fog of lust coloring my common sense—and that's when everything stopped.

In a split second, he jerked my hands above my head and pinned them against the headboard. His hands were like rings of iron, imprisoning me. He bent his head next to my ear, his warm breath, whispering against the side of my face. "No more, Hattie. This is over," he said. The words felt like a slap across my face.

"No." I didn't recognize my voice. It resembled a primitive battle cry more than a protest. "It's not over until I say it's over."

"No, that's where you're wrong. This is my game, my world. You only win what I want to give. Nothing more."

My lust exploded in a burst of volcanic rage. I kicked and bucked and everything in between, but he was stronger, easily overpowering me. Strings of curses and taunts fell like poison from my lips.

His hand cupped my mouth, smothering my rants. I bit his hand, breaking the skin, but he didn't cave. Fuck, he didn't even flinch. "Stop this. This is hard for me too. I don't want to keep fighting with you, but I will."

His eyes raked over my face with equal parts anger and violence. I believed him. He'd won. Accepting defeat, my muscles uncoiled one by one and he lifted his hand from my mouth. I sucked in giant gasps of air trying to expunge Ryker's mind games. Beat by beat my heart slowed to a normal rhythm.

"Take a shower and clean yourself up. I have a few things to do before we head back to the villa."

"If you don't want to deal with me, why did you come after me? You should've left me in the jungle. We both know I never would've made it out of there alive." Even to my ears, I sound lost. Shattered. Broken.

"You're the leverage to secure my brother's release." He shifted his body and sat up on the edge of the bed, his face turned away from me. "I'll be back in fifteen minutes. Be dressed and ready."

"My clothes are dirty." I don't understand why I said it. What I did or didn't wear was inconsequential.

"There's a change of clothes in the bathroom along with a few other toiletries." He stalked toward the door, his hands buried deep in his pockets.

"I don't want anything from you." I lied.

"Good thing I found the gun you stole from my room. I wouldn't want you to be burdened with it either."

I hurled a pillow in his direction, but it caught in netting and fell unceremoniously to the floor. "I'm not doing anything you want, not a fucking thing."

"Just shower and put on the clothes. We can

argue about what you do and don't want later." The door slammed, reverberating through the room. All my strength depleted, I sagged under the weight of my situation.

# Chapter Fifteen

Numb…that's how I felt when I slipped on a pair of too short jean shorts and a too large t-shirt. The lukewarm shower water had stung every inch of my bruised and battered skin, and as I stared into the peeling mirror, I didn't recognize the woman staring back at me.

Purple circles stained the skin under my bloodshot eyes. Red scratches marred my right cheekbone, and three butterfly bandages dotted the length of my neck. I looked like serious arm candy…just as Ricardo said. A bitter laugh escaped my mouth, startling me.

Expelling a monster breath, I exited the bathroom. I expected to find Ryker waiting for me, but he wasn't in the room. The hum of a car idling outside my window caught my attention. Maybe Ryker already left, and he planned to meet me outside.

I walked toward the open window. The rusted, three decade-old blue sedan was empty. Before I could second-guess my actions, I placed both of my hands on the window frame and threw one leg over the windowsill. For a few ticks of time that felt like an eternity; my body straddled the windowsill as my mind weighed my options, relentlessly analyzing my next move.

To hell with Ryker. I was leaving. I climbed out the window, hanging from the ledge before I jumped. My swollen ankle screamed, but I kept moving. Within seconds, I sat behind the wheel of the car. I didn't waste time. I shoved the gear into drive and slammed my foot on the gas pedal so hard I thought it might crash through the rusted metal floorboard.

Clouds of brown dust rolled upward behind the car as I drove over the gravel road. I wasn't delusional. Ryker would realize I had run again within minutes, if not seconds, but the thought didn't stop me. If Ryker wanted me, he had to work for it. Sure, he'd probably find me and punish me, but I refused to rollover and accept my fate—not when I still had viable options.

Palm tree canopies shaded the road. Green vines snaked up the tree trunks. Hints of the startling cerulean sky penetrated the green miasma. I couldn't see a damn thing, but the road had to lead me somewhere, so I kept driving. The rough dirt road combined with the never-ending twists and turns forced me to proceed slower than I wanted.

Second after second, the tires ate up the dirt road until I no longer saw the bed and breakfast in the rear view mirror. The invisible chain links around my body snapped one by one and my breath evened out. Holy shit. I was doing it. I was going to beat

Ryker and the entire Vargas Cartel with only my mind and a rusted out blue sedan. I didn't have a gun, but I had a car.

With one hand on the steering wheel, I popped the center console, searching for a map or anything that steered me back to civilization. Blindly, I emptied the contents on the seat next to me.

An empty pack of gum.

A few used tissues.

A pen.

A phone charger.

Nothing…

Leaning to the side, while keeping my eyes trained on the road, I opened the glove box, and my heart slammed against the walls of my chest. A cell phone. It was old…the kind with a flip front and barely-existent screen, but as long as it worked long enough to call a number or two, I didn't care.

My hands shaking, I opened the phone and dialed my dad's number plus the international code from memory. My dad didn't participate in the video conference yesterday, but I still thought he was my best option.

With every ring, my heart climbed the walls of my chest.

One ring.

Two rings.

"Come on…pick up." I squeezed the phone tighter and tighter.

Three rings.

"Dad, answer your fucking phone," I screamed as I white-knuckled the steering wheel with my free hand.

123

Four rings.

"Beep."

"No," I yelled.

"You've reached Richard Covington's voicemail, please leave a message."

"Dad, it's Hattie. Where are you? I need you. I'm lost. I don't know where I am." I started to disconnect the call and then I stopped. "Call me on this number," I added, hoping the number showed up on his missed calls list.

I disconnected the phone call.

My mind cataloged the people I could call. Vera. My mom. My brother. Evan. My mom and brother would be useless. Vera never answered calls from unknown numbers. That left Evan. I wavered a few seconds before I decided to call him, but in the end, I did it.

The waiting started once more.

One ring.

"Hello."

"Evan," I whispered. His name rolled off my lips like a benediction. A prayer. Even though I still hated him, he symbolized home and my life before Ryker unhinged everything I knew and believed about my life and myself. Evan cheating on me seemed like an inconsequential hiccup in comparison to my current problems.

"Hattie, baby, is that you?"

Stunned that he answered the phone, I nodded my head, forgetting he couldn't see me.

"Hattie?" he repeated louder. "Can you hear me?"

"Yes, it's me."

"Where are you?"

Fragmented thoughts tumbled from my mouth. "I don't know. I ran. I got lost. He found me. There was a bed and breakfast. We fought. Why does he do that? There was a car. I stole it, and now I'm driving somewhere. I don't know where."

"What? Hattie, you need to calm down and explain."

I slowed to a stop and surveyed my surroundings. The road dead-ended twenty feet in front of me at a small terra cotta colored cottage with a thatched roof and a light blue front door. Uneven gray stones were stacked on either side of the cottage, forming a rudimentary fence. Brightly colored clothes hung from a string between two wooden posts.

"Oh shit," I murmured.

"What?"

"I'm at someone's house."

"Don't go in," Evan warned, but his words sounded faded and distant as reality slapped me across the face.

I fled the bed and breakfast on the one road that was a dead end. No wonder Ryker didn't run after me. I couldn't go anywhere except back to the bed and breakfast, or I could get out and run aimlessly through the jungle again, because I couldn't drive the car through the dense foliage.

"I'm fucked." The words were a pained whisper ripped straight from my pulverized soul. Defeat churned savagely in my stomach, and I started to cry. I was so sick of crying. "I thought I won. I can't believe this. I can't get away from him, and

125

every time I see him I crumble."

"Who are you talking about?" Evan yelled, and I jerked in reaction to his harsh tone. I'd almost forgotten he was on the phone.

"Him." I shoved my sweaty hair out my eyes. "Oh God, Evan, I don't understand how he does it. He touches me, and I try to fight it, but he overwhelms me and I cave. I'm weak. Hopelessly pathetic. Something is wrong with me...so wrong." My voice fractured on the last word.

"Hattie, you're scaring me. What are you talking about?"

"He's corrupted me. I don't even know who I am anymore," I said, my voice sounding dead to my ears. My head dropped to the steering wheel and disjointed sobs streamed out of my mouth one after another.

"Listen to me, Hattie. I will find you. I promise. I'm sorry I hurt you. I will do whatever it takes to get you home safely, and then we'll start over. Believe me, I will never let you go again. It's you and me forever."

I wanted to believe him. I wanted my safe, predictable life so much I could practically taste it. Even more, I wanted the life I thought I had before Evan shattered it into a million pieces. "Please, Evan," I pleaded. "I need to go home. I can't stand this. I'm so confused."

"Listen to me. I'm coming for you. I *will* find you. I *will* bring you home, and then we'll start over. Together we'll create a new life until we've erased all of this shit with bigger, better, and more meaningful memories."

"Oh God, Evan, I don't know if it's possible. I'm so fucked up. This is so fucked up."

"No," Evan shouted through the phone. "Don't you dare give up on me or us, not even for a second. You have to believe you'll make it out of there."

"I can't promise anything. I don't think he'll ever let me go home again. I think he's playing me, breaking me until I'm nothing."

"No, Hattie, don't give up. You're strong. I'm strong. We'll get through this. I just need you to promise me one thing."

"What?" I whispered, wiping the waterfall of tears from my face with the back of my knuckles.

"That when I find you, you'll give me a chance to make things right between us, and we'll be together again. It'll be just like old times. You'll see."

My mind screamed at me to reject him. How could I promise him a second chance when my fate dangled from a fraying rope? When my body wanted Ryker? But that's exactly what I did. "Okay. If I ever find my way back, I'll try to give you that." I sniffed, lifting my head from the steering wheel, and that's when I saw him. Ryker stood next to the open driver's window with his arms folded across his chest.

Clumsy from fear, the phone slid out of my hand, and I screamed as the driver's side door flung open.

"Get out, now." It wasn't his appearance that made him so intimidating. It was the way he carried himself...with the grace of a jaguar. The ancient Mayans, who inhabited this area long before the

Europeans arrived, believed their kings and nobles were descended from a jaguar. And when I looked at Ryker, I believed it. He had velvet black hair, flinty predator eyes—watchful yet indifferent—and the sleek grace replicating the legends of the mythical jaguar.

"Screw you," I hissed through my locked teeth. I shook my head defiantly, but my strength withered under the intensity of his stony, gray gaze. Evan's voice echoed through the static-filled phone cradled between my legs, but the frenzied pounding of my heart drowned out his words.

Ryker picked up the phone and smashed it against the side of the car, then tossed it back into my lap. Before I could complain, he coiled his hand around my arm, yanking me out of the car with ease. My oversized t-shirt slipped from my shoulder, leaving the top of my breast exposed as he pulled me through the open car door. "Fucking hell," he said, shoving my t-shirt back up my shoulder. "Tell me who you were talking to."

"No one." I refused to make eye contact with him. Eye contact was bad. His eyes had a way of sucking all my hard fought defiance from my tattered soul.

"Look at me." He grabbed my chin and forced me to look at him. The fine hair on my nape stood on end. "Tell me," he said with a honeyed menace that chilled me to the bone.

I closed my eyes. The silence stretched, heavy and judgmental, as he waited for me to obey. Slowly, like a gathering storm, tremors erupted in my legs, moving to my torso and then my arms.

Within sixty seconds, my entire body shook with rage, fear, and dread. I fisted my hands in my shirt to regain control over my body, but it didn't help. My sanity dangled from a gossamer thread, and my chest heaved in hysterical gasps.

Ryker tightened his grip on my arm until his fingernails bit into the bruises and scratches covering my skin. "Hattie, I can't protect you unless I know everything."

I pried my eyes open, and my lips contorted with disgust. "Protect me? You're not protecting me. Every time you touch me, you rip me into a thousand pieces that I can never put back together. I'm broken. You broke me." Panic-stricken sobs tumbled from my mouth. My ears rang with the insanity, pulsing like poison through my veins.

"You don't know what you're talking about."

"Then, why don't you share what you think you know? Help me to understand," I begged incoherently as I pounded my fists repeatedly against his unyielding chest.

He captured my hands and returned them to my sides. "The less you know, the better," he said as he stroked his thumbs back and forth over the inside of my wrists.

"I won't tell anyone. I promise. If I understand what's going on, I won't try to run again. I'll do whatever you ask. Trust me."

"Hattie." His powerful body crowded me, maneuvering me backward until my tailbone pressed into the car. "Don't try to play me. You won't win." He shook his head. "Your life would be so much easier if you stopped fighting me. Haven't you learned anything yet?" he added tenderly.

Tenderness from him was dangerous. I'd seen it over and over. Any time he'd shown me mercy, I tumbled into a deeper, darker hole. Suffocating under his gaze, I wrenched my hand between our bodies and drew several sticky, damp breaths into my heaving lungs. Each molecule of air glued the pieces of my fragmented willpower back together. "Apparently not," I finally said when the ringing in my ears muted.

"Nothing is the way it seems. There are layers upon layers of things going on here. This isn't just about you. Remember that, and you'll be fine." The words fell from his mouth—low, malicious, and tainted with muddy secrets.

Already teetering on the knife-edge of control, his words shoved me over the cliff and into a never-ending abyss. Fury raged through me…hot, wild, and unhinged. A red fog tainted my vision. I wanted to kill Ryker, piece-by-piece, limb-by-limb, until he embodied the physical manifestation of my ragged mental state. I didn't care if I ever breathed another breath as long as I experienced the satisfaction of wounding him.

Revenge burned through my veins. I thought I'd spontaneously combust at any second. In one fluid movement, I lifted my knee and rammed it into his groin as my hand propelled toward his face, aiming for his eye. I missed his eye, but his knees buckled when I connected with his groin.

I didn't waste one second to study the aftermath of my burst of sudden psychosis. I darted into the jungle, trudging through green undergrowth twisting up my bare legs with every step. I wasn't stupid. He'd catch me and punish me, or worse, but I refused to become his docile pet until he discarded me however he or Ignacio deemed appropriate. Fuck that. Fuck him and his fucking layers.

With every hard-fought step, stifling, humid heat coated my skin like a wet shroud. Right then, I promised if I ever made it out of this godforsaken jungle alive, I'd never step foot out of America again. Dirt smeared my legs, and green streaks stained my clothes, but that was the least of my worries.

Ryker's footsteps echoed behind me, strong and steady, closing the distance between us with every stride. Branches snapped under my feet, and hundreds of insect legs crawled over my skin, but I didn't give up. I'd force him to struggle for every inch he gained in our battle of wills, until bone weary exhaustion haunted both of us.

Not long had passed and he was less than an arm's length away. I lunged forward putting all my strength into a singular crowning push, but he moved too quickly. Within seconds, his unyielding arms shackled my waist like thick bands of iron. The front of his body cradled my back in a simulated lover's embrace, injecting a feverous bolt of lust directly into my heart. *Damn him. Damn me. Damn this godforsaken bug infested jungle. Damn my life.*

He pressed his mouth against my ear and shivers cascaded down my damp skin. "Are you done now? How many times are we going to play this game of hide and seek?"

"Until I win," I said through panting breaths, heat already spiraling down my body straight to the apex of my thighs.

He yanked my body even closer to him and his mouth curled into what I imagined would resemble a wickedly sensual smile to the casual observer. I couldn't see it, but I felt it on the side of my face. "Hattie, baby, it's not going to happen. Wave the white flag and save both of us some time." His voice was smoky and dark, and it both tempted and repelled me.

Seething at him and myself, I opened my mouth and closed it at least two times, before I responded. "I guess we're destined to keep playing this game, because I won't give in until I'm dead or free." The strength of my words stiffened my spine, and I arched away from him.

"You don't mean that," came his velvety response as he wrenched my hips against his pelvis again. His hips rolled against mine in a scandalously erotic movement, and I whimpered, loving and hating the heat percolating between my legs from nothing more than a roll of his hips and the sound of his voice.

"No. Please don't." My control fractured second by second, breath by breath, with every brush of his hands and flex of his hips. "Let me go," I screamed. My fingers clawed at his arms and my hair whipped around my face as I frantically shook my head from side to side. I needed to get away from him before I did something really stupid like beg him to touch me again. I was one flex of his hips away from becoming his plaything. "You make me sick." I couldn't show him how much he affected me. The repercussions were unthinkable.

"Liar." In one unexpected movement, he pushed my shorts and panties down my legs and shoved me to my knees. Dirt dug into my scabbed over knees. I tried to stand up or crawl forward, but it was pointless. Ryker had one arm around my waist, imprisoning me.

"This is my game, Hattie, and until I let you go, I own you." His hand burrowed under my shirt and dove under the constraints of my suddenly too tight bra. I arched my back and pressed against the erection already straining against his zipper.

"You've ruined my life," I screamed as lust flowed like lava through my body.

Manhandling me, he rolled one of my nipples between his thumb and index finger and then pinched the over-sensitized tip. "No, your life was ruined long before you met me." He growled next to my ear like the predatory jaguar I'd imagined him to be minutes earlier. "I'm the first honest voice in your life." He clutched my hips tight, rocking them mercilessly against his erection. My anger melted into intoxicated desire.

"No, you're a bastard. I don't want anything to do with you." As the dishonest words spilled from my mouth, I cursed the traitorous throbbing sensation roaring unchecked through my nerve endings, connecting them in an intricate web of desire. His fingertip glided the entire length of my entrance back and forth and around and around, teasing me, massaging me. Moans and groans tumbled unbidden from my mouth, saying more about my sick, conflicted need for him than words ever could.

"Your mouth lies even as your body screams the truth." He slid one finger inside my pulsing sex, and my hips undulated, blooming like a flower under the warm afternoon sun. My body didn't lie. I wanted him.

"No," I said, but the word sounded more like a greedy moan than a protest. My mind had already escaped the confines of my head, flying high on the endorphins pumping through my veins. I pushed my ass against his hands, needing more than his finger. I craved the feel of him inside of me again. I'd only had him once, and alcohol clouded the memory. I needed to know if being with him was as good as I remembered, and if it wasn't, maybe I'd stop wanting him.

"You sure about that?" he questioned as he plunged another finger inside of me and then pulled it out, smearing my wetness along the outside of my sex.

"I can't—I don't know," I stammered, the haze of my desire obscuring my vision, shifting my focus inward.

"Yes or no? Do you want to feel me inside you again?" He growled, his voice rough and uncultivated. A tremor of unease coiled low in my belly, stopping me from answering, my body already told him everything he needed to know. I couldn't verbalize the treason splintering my soul.

His free hand fumbled with his belt buckle. Within seconds, his hard cock slid against my entrance, burning the last dangling thread of my inhibitions. Trembling with desire, I pushed back against him, thirsting for the rapture promised in every taunting twitch and slippery slide of his cock.

"Answer me." A cracking sound echoed through my ears as his open palm made contact with my ass. Air exploded out of my lungs and my body shook with disbelief.

"What the fuck?" I screamed, more from confusion than discomfort, as I dove forward, scrambling on my hands and knees away from him.

He lurched forward, easily capturing me before I managed to put more than a few inches between us. His fingers bit into the tender skin around my hips, so tight and punishing, he'd probably add more bruises to the black, blue, and red collage on my tattered body.

"Yes or no?" he repeated, sliding inside of me barely an inch before pulling out again.

I gasped as a jolt of pure, mind-numbing bliss boomeranged through the walls of my aching sex. Ryker played my body like Evan couldn't have dreamed of doing, and it simultaneously made me want to kill him and have sex with him. "You can't make me answer you. This is your fucking game. Play it. Show me what you've got. What's your next move, Ryker?"

His hand shot under my shirt, and he twisted my nipple, almost as though he wanted to discipline me for my defiance, or tear the words he wanted to hear from my body. Unfortunately, it only made me greedier…wetter.

"Play your role. I'm playing mine," he shot back, his voice vibrating like a lover's caress along my heated, hyper-sensitive skin. He slid the tip of his cock along my sex, never penetrating, just back and forth. With each delicious stroke, my mind buckled under the weight of my mounting desire. Awash in a madness and hunger unlike anything I'd ever experienced, any remaining decency and morality dissolved into nothingness. My future withered like a grape on a vine. I didn't care what happened to me anymore. I didn't care if he ever let me go. I just wanted him…inside me, around me, all over me right now. I could debate the consequences later.

"Then, fuck me. That's what this is about, right? You want to control me, bend me to your will. Do it."

He didn't move for one strung out second, and my mind tilted with horror. Was this another one of his mind fucks? Make me mindless with need—then walk away? My stomach flipped. White-hot fury tumbled with my desire, creating a whirlwind of rioting emotions.

"Is that a yes?" he snapped.

"Yes."

He didn't wait more than a second. He pushed inside, possessing me with one bone-jarring thrust. For a dizzying beat of time, I couldn't move. I couldn't think. I tried to catch my breath as my mind wrapped around his invasion.

"Move," I hissed through my teeth when I gathered my shattered wits.

He grunted in acknowledgment, and the vibrations rolled one after another from his body to mine as though I were an extension of him. "I like it when you're greedy."

I didn't want to answer, because right then he pulled out and thrust into me again. A prism of fireworks erupted behind my eyelids. I bit my lip trying to stifle my greedy moan, but it was too loud, and he felt too good. Hiding from reality wasn't an option.

"Did you miss this?"

"I can't miss something I only had once." It was a lie. I missed it. I wanted it. I craved it. My hips rocked back to meet his.

"Is that your way of asking me for more?" he taunted.

"Fuck you. I still hate you."

"That would make everything easier if it were true." He moved harder, faster, and my control frayed. The crude sound of our grunts and slapping skin bounced off the trees, magnifying them. Small ripples of pleasure danced through my body just out of reach, haunting me, mocking me.

Wildly seeking my release, I grinded against him. He bent over my back until his breath whispered along the fine hairs of my neck, fanning the flames of my arousal. Moans and whimpers collided, bending and twisting into a coordinated symphony of destruction. With every thrust, he moved deeper and deeper, pounding into me relentlessly. I rode the sharp edge between heaven and hell, and I was sure I'd die if I didn't come soon. I struggled against the tide of lust, toying with the idea of denying myself, but it was too much. He was too much. Some fucked up twist of fate and chemistry made me hunger for him like no other.

"Are you ready? Do you want to come?" he

whispered next to my ear through heavy pants.

Instead of answering, I moaned, nodding my head and silently praying it would be enough. He slowed his thrusts until he stopped moving and then he slid out of me. I wanted to rip my hair out. The ripples turned into tremors and then my whole body shook, craving my release like a seasoned junkie on a desperate hunt for my next fix. "Please," I said, my voice a shattered plea. "You can't stop yet. I need this. I need you." Holy shit…it was the truth. I couldn't lie. Decorum and ethics had long disappeared from the forefront of my mind.

The instant the plea fell from my perfidious mouth, he slammed inside my weeping sex in one punishing thrust that set my body ablaze as though he had never left.

"Move...damn you," I said, the endorphins clouding my brain and making it impossible to think clearly.

He chuckled, and if I didn't need him so badly, I would've clawed his eyes out.

Without missing a beat, he angled his hips, hitting the perfect spot repeatedly in a wickedly flawless rhythm. Fire and ice, love and hate, whipped through my veins. I shattered into a million unrecognizable pieces with his name bleeding from my lips and soul. Within seconds, I felt him come, wet and hard inside me, igniting another round of soul-stealing mini shocks in my core.

Angry, sated, and depleted, I collapsed onto my stomach, not even bothering to put on my shorts. Ryker won, and I lost…again. Tears stung the corner of my eyes, but I refused to set them free. They were pointless. An hour ago, I promised I'd give Evan another chance, and now I lay on the decomposing jungle floor with Ryker's come leaking from my body, staining the earth with my pathetic surrender. I didn't have a clue how to move forward. My mind plummeted into oblivion.

"Shit. Shit. Shit." I screamed, stupidity knotting my stomach when I realized I hadn't taken my birth control pill since the night I met Ryker—not that I had the opportunity. Disgust and self-loathing slithered down my spine, swallowing me in its murky embrace. I welcomed it.

Ryker didn't say a word. Not that I expected anything else. I heard the shuffle and slide of his clothes as he dressed. Distantly, I wished it was as easy for me to put myself back together again. I felt weak. Defeated. I wanted to die. Maybe he'd leave me to rot in the underbrush. I didn't think I'd care. I closed my eyes and silently prayed everything would disappear. My promise to fight Ryker had gone up in flames. The rational part of my brain told me to scrape my body off the ground and move on…persevere. I cursed my rational brain to hell. Unfortunately, Ryker sided with my brain.

# Chapter Sixteen

"Hattie." Ryker's hushed voice raked like hot coals over my skin.

"Hattie," he repeated. "Get up. We need to go."

I shook my head, leaves tangling in the strands of my hair, the smell of dirt coating my nose hairs and my chapped lips. "Leave me here," I moaned. "Just go away. I'm done."

He dragged me up by my shoulders, clamped his hand over my mouth and shoved my jean shorts into my gut. "Put on your shorts and don't say a word. Now is not the time," he hissed, scarcely a breath of air.

"Fuck you," I screamed through the confines of his hand.

"Shut up. Do you want to be killed?"

"Do it. Kill me. I don't care."

"Yes, you do." He slowly hauled me backward, his fingers cutting into my skin. I dug my heels into the dirt and strained for a nearby tree branch. He snatched my hand from the air, twisting it behind my back. "The Chechen tree is poisonous," he whispered. "Unless you want to spend the next few days in bed with a rash, I wouldn't recommend touching it."

He pulled a gun from the holster on his belt, aiming it in front of our fused bodies. Then, I spotted them…four men moving in the shadows of the trees like the four horseman of the apocalypse. They were dressed in black with red handkerchiefs concealing the lower half of their faces. AK-47-type assault weapons hung over their shoulders, and bullets draped across their bodies like morbid jewelry. Step by step, they closed in on us from every angle, strangling any possibility of escape.

"Well, if it isn't the prodigal son. I heard you were back, but I didn't believe it," one man said in a thick accent.

"Dario, long time, no see." Ryker shoved me behind his back. I clutched his black leather belt, refusing to let go of him. "Can't say I missed you."

"She's a pretty one. That was a nice performance the two of you put on," Dario said, waving his gun at me, his mercenary eyes sliding over my body. "Maybe we could pass her around. Take turns." I closed my eyes, burying my head in the middle of Ryker's back. Numb with impending horror, blood roared through my ears and my breath came in quick, short pants. I wanted to scream, but I didn't have enough air in my lungs to do anything but whimper.

"What do you want?" Ryker said.

"I'm here to take care of unfinished business."

"What unfinished business are we talking about?" Ryker sounded cool and undaunted, and not even vaguely curious, but his muscles coiled into knots next to my hands.

Dario chuckled and shook his head. "Rever's out of the picture, but even if he wasn't, it wouldn't change the future. With all his addiction problems, he can't lead the Vargas Cartel."

"Not my problem." Ryker said.

"Maybe not, but the cartel is dying. Somebody needs to take control. I'm going to be that person."

"And you think a coup is the answer?"

Dario cocked his head to the side. "It doesn't have to be a coup. I'm going to take control of the cartel assets and territories, and consolidate the power behind me. I will systematically force Ignacio to accept me as the future of the cartel."

"It'll never happen. You're a second rate hack. You don't have what it takes to run a fruit stand much less the Vargas Cartel."

Dario scoffed. "You're wrong. Unlike Rever, I've moved steadily up the ranks, working as a lookout, record keeper, plaza boss…and now it's my turn to be the head of the cartel. Do you think you can swoop in and take control like you didn't abandon us years ago to sell your soul to the highest bidder?" Dario took a half a step forward, his gun pointed at the dead center of Ryker's chest.

"I had my reasons for leaving, none of which are your business."

Dario shrugged. "You're right. As long as you're a good boy and disappear again, I don't give a shit about your reasons." Dario held out his hand. "It's four to one. You're outnumbered. You won't win this time. Hand me the gun and make this easy. I don't want to kill you. Ignacio won't like that, but I will."

Ryker paused. Tension buzzed in the air, swirling around us like a category five hurricane. "No. Not happening."

Dario took another step forward. "You can hand me the gun and live another day, or you can die now, and the animals can pick at your carcass until you're unrecognizable. It's your choice."

"Back the fuck up and leave. You're involving yourself in things you don't understand." With his gun trained on Dario, Ryker wrapped his arm around my neck and pulled my ear next to his face. "Gun. Ankle," he whispered before shoving me by the top of my head to the ground.

Dario laughed coldly, and ice crystallized inside of my veins, freezing my hand on Ryker's ankle. "No, you're the one who doesn't understand what's going on here."

Ryker pressed his leg into my hand, and I inched my hand up the inside of his pant leg never taking my eyes off Dario. I didn't understand why Ryker trusted me with a gun, but the mere fact that he did told me we were in a world of shit.

Ryker waved his gun. "Dario, what do you want? What's really going on here?"

"This is my territory now," Dario spat, waving his gun from side to side.

"Oh really? When did that happen?" Ryker's voice sounded deceivingly nonchalant, but from the short time I'd spent with Ryker, I knew he was waiting for the right instant to strike.

When I had the heavy metal grip of the gun in

my hand, I released it from Ryker's ankle holster. For a split second, I considered injuring Ryker, but then I'd be left with Dario and his murderous crew. Something told me they were infinitely worse than Ryker.

"I'm staking a claim on this territory. It should have been mine from the beginning anyway," Dario said, his dark eyebrows slashing downward, his eyes narrowing into dangerous slits. "Rever's gone, and everyone realizes Ignacio won't be around for long. I'm next in line, not you."

"Don't you think you're getting ahead of yourself?"

Dario pulled the grungy handkerchief from his mouth, exposing the lower half of his face. A sinister scar ran the length of his jaw line. "All the more reason to strike while Ignacio is down," Dario taunted.

In one fluid movement, Ryker raised his gun and pulled the trigger. A small burst of air raced over my skin. Almost instantly, Dario's body fell to the ground right next to me—his dead, lifeless eyes staring back at me, a bullet hole in the middle of his forehead.

Ryker charged forward, kicking one man in the knee, and a sickening crack vibrated through my ears as the man tumbled to the ground wailing in agony. Without pausing, Ryker swung his gun to the right, sending a volley of shots into the chest of another man. By the time he turned, the remaining gunman had a gun pressed to Ryker's temple.

"No," I screamed, surging to my feet. My entire body trembled, and the gun nearly slipped from my clammy hands. I managed to hold it in front of me—my legs spread wide, two hands cupping the grip, and one finger hovering over the trigger.

The gunman's eyes blazed like the fires of hell as he studied me. He wasn't a tall or heavy man, maybe five foot six and a hundred and sixty pounds, but evil rolled off of him in dark, ominous waves, scorching my skin with their intensity.

Time froze in a dreamlike haze as sweat trickled down the side of my face and dripped from my chin. My heart galloped erratically in my chest. It was now or never. If I didn't shoot first, the gunman would kill Ryker, and I'd be next. I sucked in a deep breath, and an unnatural calm settled through my body, infecting my mind with lethal focus.

*I can do this.*

*I can do this.*

*I can do this.*

My gun safety class freeze-framed in my mind. I pulled the gun slide back until I heard a bullet click inside the chamber. I aimed my gun at his chest. I inhaled and squeezed the trigger. The shot exploded from my gun, and I stumbled backward, tripping over a rock and tumbling to the ground. The bone-rattling impact caused the gun to fall out of my hand and skitter across the dirt.

When I opened my eyes, I saw the clear blue sky with a dusting of white, fluffy clouds. My muscles aching with lactic acid and the toxic remnants of my adrenaline surge, I strained my neck to the side as vomit rushed from my mouth in a sickening swell.

"Hattie?" Ryker crouched down next to me, an assault weapon dangling from his shoulder.

"Is he dead?" I whispered, as tiny, unrestrained tremors tore through my muscles one after another. The world around me moved in waves…in and out and back again.

"He will be in a few minutes."

I nodded instead of answering.

"I don't know if they were alone. We need to move."

"I don't feel good," I moaned, rolling to my side.

He brushed the hair off my forehead, studying my face. "I know." He held out his hand. "Ready?" No, I was too lightheaded to move, but staying put wasn't a viable option. Besides, I'd walk for days to get away from the mass murder scene in front of me.

I placed my hand in his. I didn't have a choice. Ryker was a known quantity. I knew what he wanted, or at least I thought I did. On the other hand, the other men who might or might not be lying in wait in the shadows of the trees…I didn't have a clue how they fit into the puzzle.

"Don't look," he warned, forcibly redirecting my face when my eyes darted toward the man I'd shot. He acted a second too late. The gunman was sprawled out on the ground on his back, a perfectly circular pool of blood staining his shirt, slowly spilling onto the ground mixing with dirt. The tree behind him was splattered with blood, and his eyes were fixed open, glassy with the emptiness of death.

"Walk with me," he murmured as he threaded his fingers through mine.

He led me out of the jungle and toward the dirt road where I abandoned the car I'd stolen from the bed and breakfast. With each stride, ice settled inside my bones, and I squeezed Ryker's hand tighter and tighter, strangling the circulation in his hand, but he didn't complain.

A tiny moan of despair escaped from my lips, and I shoved my fist into my mouth, digging my teeth into my flesh, trying to stop the fear from leaking out of me and draining all my strength. My reality kept turning and twisting until my old life faded from memory like a discolored, worn out photo.

Two hours ago, I hated Ryker, and I would have done anything to escape him. Now, I had tethered myself to him, never wanting to let go. He'd have to pry my cold, dead hand out of his clasp, because I refused to let him leave me anytime in the foreseeable future. He was my new obsession, my one remaining link to sanity in the insane world that had become my reality, and maybe that's what he wanted all along. I didn't care.

# Chapter Seventeen

"Shit," Ryker muttered when we reached the car. He kicked the rear passenger door. "They slashed the tires."

"We could still try to drive it," I insisted, wanting to get away from the scene of my crime as quickly as possible. I'd take solitary confinement in the relatively safe confines of the villa any day over being hunted by a mercenary band of defunct cartel members.

"Maybe on paved roads, but not on the dirt roads in the jungle." Lines bracketed his normally sensual mouth.

"We're walking?"

"Just back to the bed and breakfast if we're lucky." Ryker moved fast, practically dragging me down the dirt road by our entwined hands, but I didn't hesitate.

"What's that supposed to mean?"

Ryker didn't answer. He just shook his head.

My stomach clenched. "Tell me," I demanded. His silence scared me more than the truth. Mentally,

I needed to prepare myself for the worst.

"They probably slashed the car tires at the bed and breakfast too."

"So what? We'll be stuck at the bed and breakfast until someone comes to get us." I didn't know who that someone would be…maybe Ignacio or one of the men under his command.

"No. We can't stay there for more than a few minutes. We need to keep moving."

A shudder flitted down my spine. "Can't we call someone?"

"I don't have a phone."

"Why not?" I gaped.

"I was in a hurry to leave yesterday. Remember?" he snapped.

"So we're just going to roam through the jungle until what? Somebody finds us?"

"No. We're not going to roam anywhere. We're going to head in the direction of the villa."

"How far is the villa?"

"Approximately fifteen miles. Maybe twenty."

"If we don't have a car, we'll never make it there before dark."

"I know."

"I don't want to be stuck in the jungle tonight." I hated admitting it, but the thought of sleeping on the dirt floor with bugs and snakes didn't sound restful. I'd rather walk through the night.

"What are you afraid of?"

"Bugs and snakes," I answered honestly.

"Bugs and snakes are the least of our worries."

"What?"

"Shh," he whispered. "We're close." He paused

and I nearly slammed into his back. "We're going to walk around to the back of the building, staying just inside the perimeter of the trees."

With extreme effort, I convinced myself everything would be fine, we'd find a car in relatively good condition, and we'd be back at the villa before sunset. A moment later, we were one hundred yards from the back of the bed and breakfast. It was quiet…unnaturally quiet.

Ryker pointed to a tree stump. "Sit there. I'll be back in ten minutes."

"Wait." I clung to his hand. "I want to go with you."

"No." He peeled his hand away from mine. "You'll be safer here."

"No, I won't," I shot back, unwilling to relinquish his company for even a few minutes. I wasn't going to be the stupid girl in a horror flick, hiding alone in plain sight despite common sense.

Ryker slipped the gun from his ankle holster. "You already proved you know how to use it. Don't hesitate. Shoot anyone you see and you'll be fine. If I'm not back in twenty minutes, don't come looking for me. Follow the road on the right side of the bed and breakfast."

"Where does it go?"

"To a small village."

"Will you meet me there?"

"No. If I don't come back, I'm dead."

My mouth dropped open, and my stomach somersaulted…repeatedly. He was halfway to the back door of the bed and breakfast before I could think of a response, and even then it wasn't much of one. I curled into a ball, my back to a tree, the gun resting on the top of my knees, and my hand on the trigger.

Regardless of what Ryker expected me to do, I refused to leave him here. If I heard one flicker of a struggle or a single gunshot, I was going in. I wouldn't make it to the village or anywhere else without him. Now that he opened my eyes to the dangers of being alone, I couldn't imagine stumbling into some random village, begging for help, shelter, food, or a phone. I didn't speak Spanish beyond being able to ask for a beer or the bathroom.

Minute after minute ticked by, and my blinks became longer and longer. The humid heat and sultry jungle breeze acted like my personal lullaby, and before I knew it, I fell asleep.

I could scarcely open my eyes when warm, strong arms wrapped around my body. "So much for your future as a lookout," Ryker said as he pulled my body against his chest. I should've objected, but I was too beaten down to do anything but bury my head next to his neck.

"The tires were slashed?" I whispered against his ear.

His muscles tensed beneath my legs. "Yes."

"Damn…that sucks." I lifted my head, but he didn't look at me. He kept his eyes trained on the terrain in front of us. "What about the phone?"

"The lines were severed."

"And Ricardo and his—"

"Wife?"

"Yeah. Are they okay?"

Lisa Cardiff

"No."

"Are they," I closed my eyes and sucked in a breath. "Dead?"

"Yes."

"I'm sorry." A wave of regret slammed against my chest, thick and twisted like a wall of thorns crushing me, sucking the air from my lungs. This was my fault. All of it. From the moment I decided to go to Mexico with Vera instead of staying home and licking my wounded ego. Now countless men and at least one woman were dead because I refused to wait until Ignacio and Evan's dad finalized some stupid diplomatic prisoner swap. I whimpered as seismic shock after seismic shock rocked though my tormented body. My vision tunneled, and for an instant I thought I'd faint. It was too much to absorb.

Ryker froze mid-stride. "What's wrong?"

"Nothing."

"Don't lie to me." He released my body, and my knees nearly buckled under my weight when I hit the ground. My feet throbbed from two days of running in leather-soled sandals. "Tell me."

"This is my fault." I swallowed the nausea rumbling in my belly. "There were so many times I could've made a different decision and avoided this mess. I should've stayed home."

"You really believe that?" Ryker raised one eyebrow and folded his arms across his chest, his muscles stretching the fabric of his shirt in thick, horizontal ribbons.

"All these people are dead because of the stupid choices I made. I should've never come to Mexico.

Then, I didn't want to go to that bar where I met you, but I agreed because Vera wanted me to go. Finally, I tried to escape twice, and I didn't even do that right." I held up finger after finger until I finished my list of misdeeds and stupid decisions.

Ryker looked away for a few excruciating beats before turning his steely gaze back to me. "What you did or didn't do is irrelevant. Like I said, your future was sealed weeks before you made any of those decisions."

Squinting into the glare of the late afternoon sun, I threaded my hands through my hair and tugged at the roots. "Tell me what that means. You already said that. Tell me something new. I need to understand."

He shook his head slowly. "I can't. Let's go. We have to start walking."

"No," I yelled, my blood pressure soaring as my heart worked overtime. "Not until you tell me something...anything." He reached for my hand and yanked me toward him, but I stiffened my body, refusing to move. Granted, he could've taken off down the trail, and I would have followed him eventually. I didn't want to spend one more second alone in this jungle. I'd never tell him that, however.

He ran his hand along my cheek, and my skin tingled under the pads of his fingers. I backpedaled a few steps, but it wasn't far enough. The intensity of his gaze and his tight grasp on my hand kept me firmly in his orbit, his magnetic gravity pulling on me, making me forget everything.

"Hattie, we were coming for you regardless of

153

where you were. Mexico, your parents' house, your school campus…it didn't matter. My job was to get you here. Your trip to Mexico simplified a few things, but in the end, you'd be here."

My tongue knotted, and I couldn't form a response. The green walls of the jungle closed in on me, suffocating me inch by green inch, unraveling my sanity. My body swayed, and for a second I thought I'd collapse under the weight of my reality, but Ryker wrapped one arm around my shoulders and the other under my knees. Part of me wished he had let me fall, and god-willing, unconsciousness would have followed.

"Let me carry you for a little while. Your feet are sore, and you look exhausted," he said.

Both were true, but most of all, my mind reeled with the implications of what he said. "Why me? There are plenty of daughters and sons of high profile politicians. A lot of them are more powerful than my dad or Senator Deveron."

"You're who they wanted. Who they needed."

"Who are they? The Cartel?"

He kissed the top of my head. "They're everyone with something to lose if this doesn't succeed. Politicians. Cartels. Businessmen. You fit all their requirements. End of story."

I sucked in a deep breath and nodded, my heart shattering with doubts. I held my body rigid for a few seconds, but in the end I melted into his embrace, wrapping my arms around his neck. What more could I say? Why they picked me wasn't important. I was here, and hopefully I'd find my way home in the not too distant future.

Ryker's heart pounded sure and even next to my body, and I inhaled his scent, drawing his essence inside my lungs. For the first time in weeks, I felt like I had somebody on my side, looking out for my best interests, and protecting me...which was a dangerously delusional sentiment. He shoved a needle into my neck and abducted me. He told me I was just a job. He told me not to believe anything. But I didn't care about any of that. I didn't want to analyze the madness of my life any longer. I closed my eyes again, trusting Ryker to take care of me and grant me a few moments of comfort.

# Chapter Eighteen

The horizon had swallowed the sun about ten minutes ago, and humidity coated my clothing. With each step, my feet pulsed with a bone-deep pain that vibrated up my legs. I missed the spongy comfort of my running shoes. I missed the air conditioning. I missed the comfort of my bed. I wanted a shower, but my desires or needs weren't important. I kept putting one foot in front of the other, marching into oblivion, following Ryker through the heavily shadowed jungle. My head bowed; I studied the faintly visible contours of the path beneath my sandaled feet, trying to avoid the stones and twisted tree roots.

Just when I accepted that Ryker planned to walk until the night had faded into the haze of the orange sunrise, he halted, and I slammed into his back.

"Shh," he whispered, glancing over his shoulder.

Somewhere in the distance, I heard the faint hum of people talking and a baby crying. A flicker of fear raced down my rigid spine. I threaded my fingers through the belt loops on the back of his pants. "What is it?" I whispered next to his ear.

"It's the village."

"Is that a good thing?" My mind swirled with possibilities…both good and bad. I envisioned a cozy bed and a hot shower even though I realized both were implausible. On the flip side, I knew there was a real chance we could walk into a hostile village with more men like those we encountered earlier.

"It could be," Ryker answered. "Historically, the Vargas Cartel controlled this region, but I don't know how far Dario's influence extended."

"Dario's influence?" I echoed. "What's that supposed to mean?"

"I think Dario planned to launch an offensive against the Vargas Cartel, which means he had more than four supporters, especially since he was a plaza boss."

"What's a plaza boss?" It sounded like an important position, but I didn't know much about the hierarchy of a cartel.

"A plaza boss is the lead representative for the cartel in a particular region or town. He ensures the safe passage of a cartel's narcotics through the region, which includes making recurring bribe payments to Mexican law enforcement and local officials, and recruiting new members."

"So Dario would've had a lot of connections both in and outside of the Vargas Cartel."

"Exactly. Hopefully, he hadn't allied himself with one of the other regional cartels."

"Why?"

"Because then we'd be sitting in the middle of a

turf war, which means there could be plenty of cartel hired executioners, or *sicarios,* lurking around the area."

"Fuck," I mumbled under my breath.

"Those aren't the only potential players either. Hold this." Ryker handed me a gun. "We need to worry about the *fuerzas autodefensas* too."

"The what?"

"Self-defense forces." He laced his fingers through mine.

"Who are they?"

"They're a confederation of vigilantes that united a few years ago to fight back against the Cartels."

"That sounds like a good thing."

"Not when you're with me."

"Fuck," I said again, but the word came out fractured as it vibrated over my suddenly dry vocal cords. My heart thundered against my ribcage, and acid burned my stomach. I'd always thought the political backbiting in D.C. was rough, but it didn't compare to the complexity of stepping into the middle of a regional drug cartel war. Images of the unseen dangers creeping around me swarmed through my mind. I couldn't believe I ran away from the villa. If I had even a fraction of this information, I wouldn't have stepped foot outside of Ryker's bedroom yesterday, much less ran out the back door of the villa.

Throughout my entire undergraduate and graduate career, I had been fascinated by the motivations of different political factions. None of their motivations or history seemed half as interesting or compelling once I found myself in the crosshairs of these competing factions. I didn't give a shit what they wanted or why. I just wanted to be as far away as possible from them.

"Stay behind me." He pulled me forward step by step by our intertwined hands, but I didn't want to go in the village anymore. I couldn't even if I wanted to. My whole body tensed, muscle-by-muscle, ligament-by-ligament, bone-by-bone, rebelling against the invisible barrier marking the village ahead.

"Let's just keep walking. We'll be fine. It can't be that much longer." I leaned backward, yanking my clammy hand from his grasp.

Ryker reversed his course and turned to face me. His gray eyes narrowed and his nostrils flared. "Your feet are bleeding. You can hardly walk the twenty feet to the village, much less another couple hours.

"I won't complain, and besides, all these people and groups are probably sleeping." Shrugging, I stifled a yawn and backpedaled a few anemic steps. In a perfect world, I'd already be in bed, but my world was anything but perfect.

"Mexico's drug industry and the people caught in its web never sleep. Twenty-four hours a day, three hundred sixty-five days a year, new plants are harvested, turf wars are fought, hits are ordered, *sicarios* kill, smugglers carry loads, burros slip undetected across the border, and innocent lives are stolen for the crime of being in the wrong place at the wrong time. But if you want to keep going, we can."

"You're trying to scare me." He succeeded, but I

didn't want him to know that.

In one seamless movement, he snatched my arm and pulled my body flush against his. My heart rapid fired, pounding wildly against his chest. "Dammit, Hattie. You should be scared. Don't let go of my hand. Don't contradict anything I say or do. You're my wife. We live outside D.C. Our tour group left us behind. Neither of us speaks much Spanish. We need a place to rest for a few hours," he said, his lips a hairsbreadth from mine, the electricity that always flowed between us bursting to life.

"No way," I yelled before I could stop myself. "I'm not saying any of that." The idea of creating some altered reality, linking me to Ryker on some level beyond the present, scared the shit out of me. He'd already stolen enough of me. I didn't need further sins marking my soul, severing me from my former life and the second chance I had promised Evan. Jesus…was I really planning to run back to Evan after everything? I couldn't even begin to answer that question. I couldn't think past ten minutes, much less weeks or months into the future. I didn't know whether I had a future to bargain with anyway.

"Exactly. You won't say anything. You'll just nod as necessary."

"I can't do it. I don't like telling lies. It's not right. Let's just rest right here for an hour, and then we can move. "

He smiled, but it was frosty, and his gray eyes glittered with anger. "Haven't you learned you need to listen to me if you want to survive?" He shrugged. "But if you'd prefer to wait here where someone could discover us and do god knows what, we can do that."

My eyes widened, and I sucked in a breath. "Maybe. I'm not sure."

His eyebrows lifted. "You make the choice. I thought you'd be more comfortable in the village, but maybe I misunderstood. If you can't stand the idea of telling a few harmless lies, then we can take our chances out here with the snakes, the wildlife, and whoever else happens to wander by."

Crap. He was right. He called my bluff. I couldn't walk any more today, and I needed to get off my feet. I balled my hands into fists. "Fine, let's go. I'll say or not say whatever dumbass thing you want. I'll never see these people again. It's irrelevant." I surrendered again, but there wasn't any point to my objection. It had ended before it started. I had to rely on Ryker to do the right thing and make good choices. He knew it. I knew it. Believing I could navigate my way out of this maze alone was as smart as believing a pot of gold waited for me at the end of every rainbow.

Ryker chuckled softly, dragging his hand through his dark hair. "I thought so." Ryker slipped the strap of the assault rifle over his head and leaned it against a tree. He placed a few dead branches in front of it.

"Why are you leaving it there?" I asked.

"I doubt the people in the village will roll out the welcome mat if I have an assault weapon hanging from my shoulder. Besides, it doesn't fit with our story."

I didn't argue. Even though I felt safer when Ryker was armed, he was right. We couldn't walk into the village with weapons.

# Chapter Nineteen

The minute we crossed the invisible barrier marking the village, people stopped and stared from the windows, from their front porches…everywhere. Life in the village stretched to a halt. You would've thought a marching band had accompanied our arrival.

It was more of a town than a village. Small, adjoined white homes lined the street. A freestanding hut stood to the right with advertisements for soda painted on the crumbling light blue exterior walls. Clothes hung from clotheslines.

"*Hola*," Ryker said, lifting one hand in a hesitant wave. "*¿Habla usted ingles?*" he said to no one in particular. The words rippled through the village like a bomb. Heads turned, more people peered out their open-air windows.

After a few moments of lingering silence, a lanky man in his early twenties stepped forward. He wore dark jeans and a faded blue t-shirt. "I do," he said, shoving his hands into his pockets.

"Hi. I'm Rick, and this is my wife, Tina." My mouth dropped open. What the hell was he doing? Why didn't he tell him our real names?

"I'm Roberto."

"Nice to meet you, Roberto." Ryker held out his hand and the man shook it. "We need your help. My wife and I were separated from our tour group. Can I borrow a phone to call our hotel?"

"I don't know." The man rocked back on his heels.

"We have money." Ryker pulled out his wallet and waved five hundred pesos in front of him, which amounted to forty or fifty U.S. dollars, probably more than this guy made in a week. I cringed, imagining the entire village charging us and stealing his wallet, but I buried my doubts. I had to believe Ryker knew what to do, because I sure as hell didn't.

"*Un momento*," the man said, snatching the money from Ryker's open palm, before slipping away into a nearby house.

My eyes darted to Ryker. He smiled, wrapped one arm around my waist and kissed the top of my head in a surprisingly intimate gesture. His touch warmed and comforted me, even though I knew he did it for our audience rather than for me. I buried my head in his chest, playing the role he demanded. Unfortunately, part of me wanted it to be more than a role.

"Here," Roberto said, interrupting our embrace. He held out an old flip cell phone with hundreds of scratches and nicks. It looked as though Roberto had dropped his phone in the garbage disposal more than once. Hopefully, it still worked.

"Thank you." Ryker plucked the phone from Roberto's hand. Ryker threaded his free hand through mine and led us to the crumbling rock wall adjacent to the buildings. I trailed in his wake, too exhausted to do anything but blindly follow him, stiffness and pain settling into my joints with every step. I was dead on my feet.

"Who are you calling?" I whispered after we sat down.

"Ignacio," Ryker responded, not looking up from the phone.

The name triggered a ripple of fear through my body. I squeezed his hand, seeking a connection to him. I didn't want to see Ignacio or any of those other people again, but I didn't have a choice. Ryker must have noticed my reaction because he dropped my hand and wrapped his arm around my shoulder, pulling me closer to him. He ran his hand up and down my upper arm, lulling me into a false sense of security.

"It's me," Ryker said into the phone. I couldn't hear Ignacio's words, but I didn't have enough energy to care what he said anyway.

"I found her. She's fine. I'm fine, but we encountered some trouble today."

Ryker nodded. "Yes, Dario. You should've briefed me about that shit. He's dead, but we're stuck. We need you to come and get us. We're at that village just west of the villa. I can't remember its name." Ryker paused for a few strung-out beats. "Yeah, that's the one. See you soon," he said before disconnecting the phone.

"Is he coming?" I asked, searching his face.

"In the morning."

"What? Why?" I sputtered.

"He's not at the villa."

"Seriously?" I said, shaking my head. "Then, tell him to send someone else. We need to get the hell out of here."

He tilted his head to the side. "We'll be okay. It's not that long."

"So what are we going to do? Sit here until morning? Maybe stretch out on the dirt road and wait for someone to run us over with their donkey cart and steal your money."

"Donkey cart?" He managed a faint smile. "Don't be so dramatic. You didn't expect this to be easy. Did you?"

"I was hoping." Nothing seemed easy anymore. Even returning to my white-walled prison cell at the villa wasn't easy.

"Maybe you'll stop running then."

"I'm done running," I answered, but then he smirked, pissing me off. "For now, Rick," I amended using the fake name he gave Roberto.

He laughed. "Sure thing, Tina."

"Ugh. I hate that name. Couldn't you have used my real name?" I drew circles in the dirt with the tip of my dusty sandal.

Ryker's smile faded. "No. People are looking for you...for me." He stood up. "Let's see if I can negotiate a place to stay until morning."

He didn't grab my hand or wrap his arm around me this time, and I hated that I noticed his lapse. "I'll wait here," I said sullenly.

"Fine."

Five minutes and a few exchanges of money later, Ryker returned. "We have a place to sleep."

"Five star accommodations, I assume," I said, pushing my body off the rock wall. "I'd kill for some air-conditioning, a shower, and five hundred thread count sheets." I sounded like a bitch, but I didn't care. "A change of clothes would be nice too."

"I can only promise you a bed. The other stuff will have to wait until you get home. Maybe Evan can take you on a vacation when you're released, and he can treat you to all the stuff you're missing."

"Evan?" I questioned, my heart sputtering inside my chest.

"That's who you were talking to on the phone when I found you." His jaw twitched, and anger flashed across his face, contorting his even features.

The air around me stagnated as I searched the suddenly blank slate of my mind for something to say. "How did you know?"

"I heard you." He rubbed his hand over the dark stubble coating his cheeks.

"What did you hear?" I shifted my head to the side, pretending I didn't care what he did or didn't hear, that I didn't have anything to hide, that my heart wasn't about to split my ribcage in half.

Ryker moved forward, dropping his hands on my shoulders, and pulling my body against his. "Are you playing games? We both know what you said. Don't act like you can't remember."

"Games?" I echoed, frozen in the prison of his loose embrace. To everyone in the village, we probably looked like a happily married couple sharing a tender moment, but hostility crackled between us.

"You said you're going to give Evan another chance." Danger and maybe jealousy glittered in his dark eyes. No, it couldn't be jealousy. Ryker didn't care what I did with Evan. We both knew this thing between us ended the minute he released me.

"I said I'd try. I didn't promise it'd work."

He reached up and brushed his hand through my short hair, tugging lightly on the tangled strands. "You shouldn't have called him. It complicated things."

"You don't know that." Even as I said it, my stomach revolted with the truth. It probably did complicate things. I told Evan I had escaped, and then he heard Ryker. Evan was likely crazed with worry, not to mention my friends and family.

"Don't play dumb." He brushed a kiss across my forehead...probably for our audience. The tips of his fingers trailed up my neck and then he cupped my face. "I was in the middle of negotiating a prisoner swap. When my prisoner escaped, I lost my leverage."

"Evan probably heard you, so he knows I didn't go far."

"You're wrong," Ryker replied shaking his head. "Ignacio said negotiations have stalled until I can produce your pretty face for a live video conference again."

I tore my face from his grasp. "Great. Another reason Ignacio should've sent someone to get us tonight."

"No, that's another reason you won't defy me again. Every rebellion equates to more days before you can go home."

"Home," I whispered.

"Yes, home. You're going home soon as long as you listen to me."

"I know." And I did, but part of me didn't want to let him go…yet. In one of my college psychology courses, I'd learned that some kidnapping victims developed a bizarre bond with their jailer as part of the victim's psychological survival defense mechanism. I think my professor called it traumatic bonding. Maybe I could attribute my growing attachment to Ryker to a simple trick of human psychology, which meant my feelings would fade with time and reflection. Part of me wanted that to be true, and part of me mourned the impending loss of my connection with Ryker. I rubbed my hands over my face. I was broken…well and truly broken. Dammit.

"I'm glad we understand each other," he said before he scooped me up into his arms. "Let's get some rest."

Ten minutes and as many Spanish greetings later, Ryker set me down on a narrow bed. I didn't waste a second before I pulled the brightly colored blanket over my body. Nubby balls covered the sheets, and the blanket scratched my already bruised and battered skin. Even camping in a sleeping bag would have been better, but at that moment it felt like heaven. I could sleep for days. I rolled to my side and tucked my hands under my pillow, my eyes already heavy with sleep.

Ryker closed the flimsy door and secured the hook and eye latch, not that the flimsy metal contraption would bar anyone from entering. It might slow them down a fraction of a second.

He sat down on a pine rocking chair in the corner, removed his black leather loafers and slipped the gun out of the holster under the hem of his shirt. "Do you want me to turn off the light?"

"Yes. Do you want the blanket?" I asked, realizing he didn't have anywhere to sleep.

"No." He flipped the light switch, and I couldn't see anything, but I felt Ryker. Every inch of my skin prickled as he moved closer and closer to me. The bed dipped as he sat on the edge of the bed. I rolled away from him, trying to ignore his nearness, which was easier said than done. Then, he slipped under the blanket next to me, cocooning me in his embrace, and I couldn't ignore him regardless of how hard I tried.

"Why are you in bed with me? It's too small." I tossed his arm off my body, but he didn't even hesitate for a second before clamping his arm around my waist again, tethering me to him even tighter than before.

"It's better than the floor."

"But I'm using it."

"So am I," he answered. "Now, be quiet and go to sleep while you have the chance. At this point in time, I don't have an ulterior motive, but I could always change my mind."

"Fine. But keep your hands in a safe zone," I warned.

He slipped his hand under my shirt, his fingertips

less than an inch from my breasts. I sucked in a breath. "Is this a safe zone?" he said, his warm breath skimming the side of my face.

"No, it's a gray area, and gray areas are off limits too." I needed to sleep, and I didn't trust myself around him. If he kept this up, I'd become the aggressor.

"How about here? Is this still a gray area?" he asked as his hand traced the underside of my breast.

"Not a safe zone and you know it."

He chuckled, moving his hand to the outside of my shirt. "I was just teasing you."

I sighed irritably. "You're evil."

"But you like it when I misbehave, and I'd hate to disappoint you."

He rolled over, pinning my body beneath his, bracing his weight with his arms. His gazed drifted to my mouth, lingering there for a drawn out heartbeat. I'd never wanted to feel his lips against mine more than at that instant.

"I shouldn't kiss you."

I nodded, the back of my head sliding against the nubby pillowcase. "No, you shouldn't," I agreed, even as I burned with the need to taste him again. If he didn't kiss me, I had every intention of kissing him.

"But I'm going to do it anyway."

"I know."

The tips of his fingers tunneled into the tangled strands of my hair, and he brushed a feather-like kiss across my lips. My heart seized, but it wasn't even close to enough. I arched into him, and within seconds our lips fused to together, hot and heavy.

I sunk into him, into his kiss, moaning when his tongue slipped past my lips. I kissed him like my life depended on it, and maybe it did.

I tasted him.

I inhaled him.

I clung to him.

Dizzy and lightheaded, my body shook with unrestrained desire, and I couldn't get enough. Remotely, I registered the shuffling of feet and whispered conversations in the hallway, but I didn't care. My mind didn't have room for anything except the wicked caress of his tongue against mine and the ache building inside of me.

And then he stopped, his lips hovering over mine, his exhalation becoming my inhalation. The pad of his thumb traced my lower lip, and time grinded to a halt. His gray eyes searched my face, then he pressed a kiss to the tip of my nose.

"Goodnight, Hattie," he whispered before rolling over and swaddling me in a side-by-side embrace.

I told myself to object and shove him off the bed, or beg for more, but I couldn't summon the words or willpower to do either. He felt too good, too warm, and too safe. So instead, I closed eyes, drew his spicy, sea salt infused scent into my lungs, and fell asleep.

# Chapter Twenty

A knock on the louvered wood door woke me early the next morning. My eyes fluttered around the room, taking in my surroundings. Yellow stains dripped down the empty, white walls. Ryker's heavy arm circled my waist. Springs burrowed into my side from the thin mattress. Light poured into the room around the edges of the faded, cornflower blue curtains. For a split second, I couldn't remember where we were, but then I heard Ignacio's voice.

"Ryker, are you in there?"

A night of sleep had centered my thoughts and erased the spiraling panic etched in my mind, but the moment I heard Ignacio's voice, my muscles tensed and my stomach soured.

"Shit," Ryker mumbled as he rolled onto his back and dropped his hand over his eyes.

"Ryker?" Ignacio said again, his voice echoing off the walls. The door handle jiggled, and the hook and eye latch threatened to snap under the pressure.

"I'm coming." Ryker sat up, his feet hanging

173

over the side of the bed.

I scrambled off the bed and leapfrogged to the far corner of the room, putting as much distance as possible between the door and me. My tattered sandals were on the side of the bed. Slipping my feet into them for another day sounded like a rare form of torture. A large blister lined the heel of my right foot, and the constant abrasion from the leather strap between my first two toes had left my skin raw. Transiently, I considered leaving them for the owner of the house, but I didn't have many shoe options at the villa, so I picked them up.

"Get up," Ignacio barked. "Dario was working with the Alverez Cartel. We need to leave before someone sells us out and we have to fight our way out."

Ryker shoved his feet into his shoes and stalked toward the door. His dark hair stuck up at different angles, and the side of his face had indentation marks from the sheets. Pausing with his hand on the lock, he glanced over his shoulder. "Don't tell anyone what happened between us." He had lowered his voice until it barely reached a whisper.

"Who would I tell?"

Ryker ran his hand through his hair and his mouth tightened. "Ignacio. Everyone. Fuck…I don't know. Just keep it to yourself. It was a mistake. It can't happen again. Ever."

Unreasonable and wholly unwarranted pain burst through my heart. I agreed with him. What happened between us was a mistake so many times over. Ryker was my jailer. I promised Evan a second chance. Ryker lived in a violent world beyond my comprehension—one I'd never understand. Sadly, none of that made a difference to my sick and twisted heart. I was ten kinds of a fool.

"Hattie?" Ryker prompted when I didn't answer him, his gray eyes searching mine. "Did you hear what I said?"

"Why?"

He pinched the bridge of his nose. "To protect you. That's all I can say."

I squeezed me eyes shut, trying to find comfort in his words. "And pushing me away and pretending nothing happened will protect me?"

"Yes." He sighed. "This is the way it has to be. This is the way it should have been."

"Fine. I won't tell anyone, ever," I mumbled, turning my head to avoid his gaze. Instead, I stared blindly at the walls of the room, willing the numbness to take over so I didn't feel anything. I used to do the same thing as a kid when my mom's demands became too much. It helped me survive in the past, and I needed it now for the same reason. Within mere seconds, I relaxed as the familiar blanket of nothingness rolled through me.

"Good. Are you ready?"

With little reluctance, I shuffled toward the door. "I guess so," I replied, because what else could I say? I didn't want to go back to my windowless cell, but I didn't want to stay here either. I could scream and cry about the unfairness of my life later. Right now, I didn't have a choice. I had to keep moving forward and embrace the nothingness until I could reclaim my life.

Ryker unlatched the lock. "Do I need to tie your

hands or will you follow me willingly?"

Dropping my sandals to the floor, I balled my hands into fists in front of my body. My fingernails dug into my palms. "Do whatever you want," I mumbled, resisting the urge to fight him even as anger sparked in my veins, swallowing my numbness piece by piece. "I followed you all day yesterday, and I didn't try to leave last night, but it's your call."

Lines bracketed the sides of his mouth as he pressed his lips into a firm, straight line. "Let's go then." He wrenched the decrepit door open, and there stood Ignacio.

His dark eyes flashed between Ryker and me. The skin at the corners of his eyes crinkled into deep lines. I wished he wouldn't look at me that way. It made me feel exposed...transparent.

"Is everything okay?" Ignacio asked, running his tanned hand through his salt and pepper hair.

I'd never noticed the resemblance between him and Ryker until that moment. While I suspected Ryker looked more like his mom than his dad, he had his dad's long, angular nose, heavy-lidded eyes, and broad shoulders.

"Everything is perfect. Miss Covington agreed she wouldn't run again, so we shouldn't have any additional problems before it's time to make the exchange." Ryker folded his arms across his chest, but he didn't turn around to look at me. Damn him and his calm ambivalence.

"That's what you said when you left her in your room alone and without a guard," Ignacio shot back.

"She won't run again," Ryker retorted without

any further explanation. "Right, Miss Covington?"

I stared at the ceiling, studying the web of hairline cracks, extending outward in a maze from the white ceiling fan. I hated surrendering so easily, but it was true. I wasn't running again unless Ryker happened to stop in front of the U.S. embassy, and I wouldn't hold my breath for that to happen. "No," I answered after a heavy pause.

Ignacio scanned the disheveled bedding. "It's not a good idea to get involved with the cargo."

"Cargo?" I said.

Ryker glanced over his shoulder at me, his eyes cold as ice even as a chuckle fell from his deceptively seductive lips. "In the world of cartels, cargo is a hostage. Targets are execution victims."

"Hm." At least Ignacio didn't call me a target. I might become one at some point, but not yet.

"Is there anything I need to know?" Ignacio persisted.

"I don't have anything to share. Miss Covington, do you?" Ryker's question was so innocent, so utterly lacking in guile that I knew he intended to bait me.

"No," I whispered, dropping my eyes to the ground, flames of embarrassment warming my face. My gut twisted. He asked me to pretend nothing happened between us…that he didn't cradle me all night. Fine. I could do that. I mentally scrubbed his scent and the specter of his touch from my skin.

"Great. Put your sandals on and let's get out of here. I'm tired from trekking through the jungle for two nights." Ryker said, stepping to the side, signaling for me to go out the door first.

I stuffed my feet into my sandals with far more enthusiasm and energy than I'd thought possible given the rollercoaster of emotions circling in my mind. Just when I thought Ryker and I had managed to form some semblance of a truce and mutual trust, he turned into an asshole again. Even though he had protected me, killed for me, lied for me, and carried me when my body failed me, I felt invisible and insignificant under his indifferent gaze. We agreed not to tell anyone what happened between us, but I didn't appreciate his cruelty. I wouldn't cry, though. I had already indulged in enough self-pity for a lifetime.

Hot, cold, fire, ice...I didn't know what to expect from Ryker anymore. One minute, I believed we had a connection. The next, he made me feel like less than nothing. He broadcasted hundreds of mixed messages. I debated whether he suffered from a bipolar disorder. Screw it. Dwelling on him longer than I already had was senseless.

Ryker promised I would be home soon, and I decided to focus on that. Once I was safely in my bed at home, I owed it to myself to cry, scream, and do all of the self-destructive things I wanted...until I erased all the contradictory emotions I harbored toward Ryker from my system forever.

"Do you have your gun?" Ignacio asked Ryker the minute we stepped out the front door of the small house we'd slept in last night.

Ryker lifted the hem of his shirt, flashing his gun.

"I thought you left that on the nightstand last night."

"I did, but then I put it back on after you fell asleep."

"Did you sleep with it loaded?" I blurted out.

"Yep."

"It could've discharged while we were sleeping."

"I'm a professional, Miss Covington. Don't worry about me," Ryker said mockingly, his eyes unnervingly distant. He treated me as if I were the dumbest person in the world, and maybe I was, or at least when it came to him. He charmed me, kissed me, fucked me, and then dropped me cold every single time—but I still couldn't muster the willpower to do anything except follow in his wake like a lost puppy. What was wrong with me?

I didn't bother responding, neither with words or a facial expression. He didn't want to talk. He wanted to pretend like I meant nothing. Fuck him. When we reached the street, six black SUVs idled next to the curb. At least ten men dressed in fatigues stood beside unopened doors. Just like the gunmen yesterday, they were armed with assault weapons, except these men also wore flak jackets with FEDI inscribed across their chest.

"What does FEDI mean?" I asked Ryker.

"*Fuerzas Especiales de Ignacio*, or Ignacio's Special Forces."

I guess that explained why the town inhabitants hovered near the doors of their homes and businesses, gawking at the Vargas Cartel's show of force. Regret twisted in my gut. I hated that I played a part in lying to these people, and in doing so, I had invited the Vargas Cartel into their small town. Who knows what sort of atrocities they had

# Lisa Cardiff

committed here? I'm sure the Vargas Cartel had victimized someone's son, daughter, or husband. I didn't know a lot about the Mexican drug wars, but I did know it had claimed thousands of innocent and not so innocent lives.

I kept my head buried against my chest, avoiding the curious and accusing stares burning up every inch of my exposed skin. Ryker slipped into the front passenger seat of the first SUV. I reached for the door handle of the same vehicle.

Ignacio snagged my wrist. "No. You're driving with me."

My eyes darted to Ryker, but he slammed the door without acknowledging me. I swallowed back my fear of being alone with Ignacio, and I nodded.

Guiding me down the uneven sidewalk, Ignacio opened the back door of the next vehicle and gestured for me to get in.

# Chapter Twenty~One

Ignacio didn't utter a single word for the first ten minutes of the drive back to the villa. Part of me should've appreciated his silence, but I knew he had something to say, and waiting for him to start talking rattled my nerves. If he wanted to yell at me, interrogate me, or hurt me, I wished he'd go ahead and do it.

Turning my head toward the window, I watched the blurred landscape as the car ate up the distance. I concentrated on keeping my breathing even and my mind clear. Ignacio had ruled the Vargas Cartel for a long time. He knew exactly how to torture me without saying a word or lifting a finger. Waiting for his judgment tangled my nerves and transported me on a horror-filled journey of what-ifs.

"I'm sorry I cut your neck. At the time I believed it was necessary, but I don't like that it happened. I don't like to hurt women."

I turned to face him so fast, I probably had whiplash. "What?" I said, because I couldn't think of anything else to say. I had a few theories about why he wanted me ride in the car with him, but an apology certainly wasn't one of them.

"I'm sorry," he repeated. "I did it to make a point, but I should have found a different way to do it…one that didn't involve physically harming you. Hurting you wasn't part of the plan."

"Okay." I tapped my fingers on the gray leather seat, trying to release some nervous energy. "Thanks, I guess."

"As a parent, I would do almost anything for my children."

I nodded, but I didn't answer. What the hell did he expect me to say—that I forgave him for orchestrating my abduction because he wanted to rescue his son? Not fucking likely.

Ignacio shifted in his seat. "I couldn't let Rever rot away in an American prison, regardless of what he did. For better or worse, I love him unconditionally. Ryker too."

"What did he do?" It wasn't my business, but I wanted to know the crime he committed. My comfort and my future were being sacrificed to resurrect his freedom. In my opinion, that sacrifice entitled me to something.

"He was arrested in Las Vegas for money laundering."

I snorted. I couldn't help it. The charge was hardly surprising or unexpected. Of course he was arrested for something related to the criminal activities of the Vargas Cartel. Ignacio's words led me to believe he did something else—something unforgivable. "That's what happens when you launder money for a drug cartel. How did he get caught?" "

"He exchanged fifty million dollars for a gambling credit in a casino on the Strip. He lost forty percent of it. The casino returned half of his losses in the form of luxury cars and gifts, then cut him a check for the balance of his gambling credit," Ignacio answered, curling his hands into fists beside his pants.

My eyes widened. "Seriously? That really works?"

"It's a method cartels have been using to clean dirty money for years."

"But you lose millions."

Ignacio rubbed his thumb and forefinger along his chin. "Most cartel members think of it as a tax of sorts. We help the casino's bottom line. They help us legitimize the money."

"Wow," I muttered, utterly dumbfounded because it was almost brilliant in its simplicity. "Impressive."

"Unfortunately, it wasn't his money. He stole the money from me...from the Vargas Cartel. He betrayed his family, his history, his heritage, and my legacy. He wanted to start a new life. He didn't like being under my thumb, so he threw us away like we meant nothing to him."

I shrugged, even as the intensity of his heavy-lidded stare burned up my skin. "Well, good for him. He succeeded. It sounds like he found his new life... a justified prison term. What's he looking at? A life term?"

Ignacio slammed his hands on the leather seat. "I won't let the U.S. government determine his punishment. It's not their job. It's mine."

"Fine. Then, go get him, but leave me out of your plans. I didn't steal your fucking money. I didn't shit on the Vargas Cartel and its criminal legacy. I'm just a graduate student with a dad who has an important job. That's it. I don't deserve this. I want my life back."

"Exactly. You're the woman with a dad who can wave his bureaucratic wand and make all my problems—and the problems of some very important people—disappear."

Frost coated my veins. "What important people?"

"People who don't want Rever to leak their connections to the Vargas Cartel."

My mind raced with the implications of his confession. "What kind of people? Corrupt politicians?" I speculated. Who else would orchestrate something like this? I wasn't naïve. I grew up in D.C. I heard fragments of hushed conversations in shadowed rooms. Some politicians had as many connections with criminal organizations as they did with lobbyists, unions, and government officials.

"So cynical," Ignacio chided. Then, he grinned. "But you're on to something, though it goes much deeper than that."

"What am I? Collateral damage? You don't care you're ruining my life to get what you want, just like you ruin innocent people's lives with the drugs you smuggle into my country. All for what?" I raised my hands in the air. "To line your pockets with dirty money built on the destruction of countless lives."

His eyes combed over my body, studying me, analyzing me…judging me. My mom knew how to stare down her nose with the best of them. I channeled her. I became her. I narrowed by eyes. I tipped up my chin. I pursed my lips. I curled my hands into a tight fist, refusing to blink, refusing to look away. I demanded respect. In that flash of time, he was my overlord. He could do whatever he wanted with me, but I wouldn't cower. I wouldn't bend.

"Collateral damage," he whispered, almost as though he tasted the words as they rolled over his tongue. "Interesting choice of words."

I raised my eyebrows and lifted my chin. "How so?" I shouldn't argue with him. He could kill me any second, but I was tired of accepting my fate. I wanted answers. I deserved answers. Ignacio probably didn't agree, but I needed to try.

He raised his open palms in the air with a faint smile on his face. "The United States and Mexico have a unique relationship. The countries share one of the longest borders in the world, stretching nearly two thousand miles, and they also share a narcotics problem. Mexico is one of the largest suppliers in the world, while the United States is the largest consumer. As long as the demand exists, the supply will be met. It could be my cartel, or another one servicing the demand. It's irrelevant. If we don't do it, somebody else will. The addicts are collateral damage…just like you."

I glared at him, and my body shook as outrage spiraled through me, twist after twist, each one hotter and wilder than the previous one. "And you don't care that those drugs ruin people's lives? That you've built an empire on the backs of the lives you've destroyed?" I challenged.

"I don't ruin lives. Bad choices ruin lives."

"But you give them the ability to make a bad choice." I corkscrewed my fingers in the hem of my shirt.

"They use drugs to fill some hole in their life. I didn't put that hole there. Drug addiction is the symptom of a deeper problem."

I folded my arms across my chest. "Great. Wash your hands of any moral responsibility."

He chuckled, sounding way too much like Ryker. I didn't want to see any similarities between this cruel drug lord and the man my heart and soul craved even though my mind knew it was wrong. "Speaking of moral responsibility, what's going on between Ryker and you?"

Heat flooded my cheeks, and my heart skipped a beat or two. "I don't know what you're talking about."

Ignacio smiled. "Ryker and Rever have different mothers. Did he tell you that?"

I sucked my lower lip into my mouth, debating how to answer this, but in the end I decided it was irrelevant if I told him the truth. Ryker would likely tell him everything and anything he wanted to know anyway. "Yes."

"Ryker was the product of an affair. He spent the summers with me, but for the most part his mother raised him. I raised Rever, though. From his first breath, I groomed him to be my successor. I focused all of my efforts on ensuring Rever would be ready when I wanted to retire. Ryker was an afterthought. I love him. My blood flows through his veins, but I poured all of my blood, sweat, and tears into shaping Rever."

"I don't understand what any of that has to do with me," I said when he stopped talking.

"Just that Ryker has worked hard for everything he's achieved—"

"A career as a kidnapper. Is that your idea of achievement?" I mocked, interrupting him. "I can see why you have one kid in jail and the other on his way."

"You don't know what you're talking about, so I'll overlook your disrespectful comment," Ignacio snapped. "All of them."

"Then enlighten me," I challenged.

Ignacio glanced out the window. "No. You don't need to know anything, except that there's a lot going on beneath the surface here. If you want your life back, you need to keep to yourself, and stay away from Ryker. Everything will be over within the next few days."

"Stay away from Ryker?" I repeated robotically. "Why?"

His head snapped toward me, his black as coal eyes blazed with anger, and his hands curled into fists beside his legs. "Because I don't need whatever the fuck is going on between you and Ryker to screw up everything I've worked for over the last decade."

"He doesn't care about me. He can barely stand to be in the same room as me. You don't have anything to worry about," I muttered, even though a small part of me believed Ryker did care. I wanted him to care.

He stroked his hand back and forth over his lips, contemplating and evaluating his next words. After an extended beat, he dropped his hand into his lap. "That's not what it looked like on the video."

"Excuse me?"

He cocked his head to the side. "I'm sure Ryker intended to delete the video, but then you ran, so he didn't get the chance."

"What video?" I asked, but I suspected the truth. I knew exactly where this conversation was headed. I should've shut my mouth and let the suspicion remain a suspicion rather than forcing Ignacio to validate it with words.

*Stupid me.*

His black as night eyes burned into mine, and his lips ticked up just a notch, or maybe I imagined it. "The one from the bathroom after our video conference with Senator Deveron and your lovesick suitor."

Blood roared through my ears, and my vision tunneled. That video was a travesty on so many levels. My mind refused to wrap itself around the implications, both future and present. That video would hang over my head for infinity, and I'd be a puppet dancing to Ignacio's tune to avoid exposure.

My life in politics…gone.

The possibility of any future with Evan…gone.

Any position of significance, doing anything I loved…gone.

Ignacio had taken the shattered pieces of my life

and tossed them in my face like confetti. Jerking my head from side to side, I reined in my runaway thoughts. "You have cameras in your son's room? Don't you trust him?"

Ignacio folded his arms across his chest and studied my face before he responded. "I don't trust anyone—not my sons, not my business partners, and certainly not spoiled rich girls. You don't get far in my world on trust. You need power, money, weapons, and cunning."

"What are you going to do with the video?" My voice came out strangled and rough even to my ears.

"Nothing right now. Stay away from Ryker, and I'll make sure it's destroyed. If not…" He shrugged. "Who knows? Maybe I'll send it to Senator Deveron's son as a Christmas gift or an engagement gift if you patch things up with him."

The car stopped in front of the villa. "Perfect. Then I'll use evidence to prosecute you and Ryker," I bluffed. I didn't have any leverage. He knew it. I knew it. My threat was empty.

Ignacio smiled, but it didn't reach his eyes. "That will be an interesting conversation. I wonder how they will interpret the video." He ran his finger across his pursed lips. Then, he opened the car door, and for an instant I thought he was done with our conversation. "Maybe they'll think you collaborated with your lover to secure the release of his brother."

My body went deathly still as his comment reverberated through my mind. "They wouldn't…they couldn't," I whispered, but I realized it was a real possibility. I'd have a lot of explaining to do if anyone from my life saw that video.

He reached across the backseat and squeezed my thigh. "Now that I think about it, I'm impressed by Ryker's ingenuity. He didn't discuss this with me, but it was a brilliant move. He turned the victim into a co-conspirator, thereby insuring your silence." He stepped down from the car without looking back. "Ryker will accompany you to your room."

Speechless, I didn't say anything as I watched Ignacio march up the steps of the monster-sized villa. He left me alone, gambling I wouldn't run again. But what was the point? They had the video, which meant I was along for the ride, regardless of where it took me. Granted, I already decided I wouldn't try to escape, but the video cemented my compliance.

This was my new reality. For better or worse, my fate was intertwined with Rever's, a man I didn't know—a man who had lost his battle with the Vargas Cartel too.

Sunlight streamed into the car through the open door, replacing the cool air with the sticky humidity I'd become accustom to over the past two weeks. Conversations in Spanish hummed outside my door, but I didn't care what was being said. For the first time since Ryker had taken me, I didn't even try to pick out words I recognized.

Was I really supposed to receive my graduate degree in two months? Did I really secure that internship at the International Foreign Policy Council? Did I really think I could slip back into my old relationship with Evan like nothing had happened?

In one impulsive second, I tossed it all away. And for what? A flash in time with Ryker—a man who offered nothing. Promised nothing. A million explanations filtered through my mind that I could offer the authorities to justify the images on the screen.

That I suffered from Stockholm syndrome.

That someone held a gun to my head.

That I had been drugged.

But I'd know the truth. It haunted me. It tortured me. I was addicted to Ryker. I would never say no to him. Not today. Not tomorrow. Not three years from now. I wanted him, even though I knew wanting him was wrong.

I couldn't help it.

I couldn't stop it.

I didn't want to.

Yes, Ryker knew about the cameras. Yes, I'm sure he realized we were being recorded. Yes, that was probably part of his plan. And yes, the video threatened my ability to recapture my future…a future I didn't even know if I wanted anymore. None of it seemed as real as what I felt for a man I loved to hate and hated that I loved. It was a demoralizing, gut-churning conclusion that had me curling into my seat of the car.

No, not my seat.

Ignacio's seat.

Ignacio's car.

Ignacio's driveway.

Ignacio's house.

Ignacio's video.

I was surviving on the charity of a man known for his cruelty, a man who had just threatened to destroy me.

I had officially hit the bottom. My life was broken. I was broken. Every fucking thing was broken. Shattered. Destroyed. I couldn't even pretend otherwise.

# Chapter Twenty~Two

"Do you want to go inside or do you plan to sleep in the car?" Ryker asked leaning inside the backseat of the car, his hands braced against the doorjamb.

"Did you know?" I asked, my mind still reeling with the implications of the conversation with Ignacio. I didn't know how long I'd sat, unmoving in the backseat of the car with the door still open. When I scanned the exterior of the villa, I noticed that everyone had long since gone inside.

He cocked his head to the side, and his eyes drifted over me. Undoubtedly, I looked like a wreck. I felt like one, both mentally and physically.

"About what?" he asked.

My eyes fell to my lap, and I ran my finger along the frayed hem of my too long t-shirt. "About the video?"

"The video conference with your father scheduled for tomorrow morning? Is that what you're talking about?"

My eyes flickered to his as I chewed on my

lower lip, rolling it between my teeth. "No." I cleared my throat, piecing together the courage to ask the next question. "The one of us together in your bathroom." Waiting in frozen silence, I momentarily stopped breathing.

His eyes widened. "Fuck." He slammed his hand against the outside of the car. The hollow metal sound echoed through my ears. "Fuck," he said again, as he pushed away from the door and took a few steps back, his body rigid, his nose flared. "I knew there was a camera in the bathroom. There are cameras everywhere. Ignacio records everything…everyone."

"Is that why you…you…" I scrubbed my hands over my face. "It that why you were with me? So you could blackmail me later?"

Ryker shook his head. "No."

I scooted toward the opening, dangling my legs out the side of the car. "Then why?"

He stalked toward me and dropped his hands on my thighs. A spark of anger mixed with arousal ignited under his hands and I shivered one long, traitorous shiver that traveled the length of my spine.

"Tell me," I whispered, swallowing over the growing lump in my throat. "I need to know, because Ignacio said—"

Shadows flashed through his silvery gray eyes. He covered his hand over my mouth, interrupting me. "I did it because I wanted you, but we can't go there anymore, Hattie. I already told you it was over. We made a mistake. I planned to erase the video the night you left. I was waiting for Ignacio to go to sleep, but I didn't do it because you ran before I had the opportunity."

My breath whooshed out of my chest and I swayed toward him, bringing my lips only inches from his. I knew I couldn't kiss him or touch him ever again, so I closed my eyes for a split second as I shook my head. "Ignacio plans to use the video against me. He's going to ruin me, my life…everything."

"No, he won't." His fingers dug into my thighs.

"How do you know?"

"Because I won't let him." He withdrew one of his hands from my legs and rubbed the back of his neck.

"Can you control him?" Stupid question—I know. Of course he didn't have any leverage to control Ignacio. Ignacio was his boss of sorts. His fucking father. Still, my eyes searched his, silently begging him to contradict me.

"He'll do what I tell him to do." His tone was solid, definite, and full of confidence. Was it misplaced? I didn't know.

"How can you say that?"

"I don't work for him."

"But…" I ran my hands through my hair, tearing my fingers through the tangled strands.

"Look, Hattie, I can't tell you everything, but I promised you could go home and you'd get your life back, and that includes walking away without a video or any other incriminating evidence hanging over your head."

I sat unmoving for a second, waiting for him to add to his explanation. He didn't. He wouldn't, but he'd given me all the reassurance I needed. "Okay," I said feeling relieved, but also feeling like an idiot for believing in him.

"Come on. Let's check out your new room." He held out his hand. I slid my hand into his and hopped out of the car. I didn't want to let go of him. He was the only solid thing in my life, but he didn't give me the choice. He dropped my hand the minute my feet hit the pavement—one more symbolic gesture pointing to his imminent departure from my life.

"New room?" I questioned, following him toward the villa instead of the shack-like structure he put me in when I arrived the first time.

"Yes. I arranged for you to have a room in the villa." He glanced over his shoulder. "Next to mine so I can check on you from time to time, but for the most part, you'll be free to roam the villa and its grounds."

Surprised, I stopped walking. "I can go wherever I want. No one will stop me?"

Ryker turned to face me. "As long as you don't do anything stupid, you're free to stay in your room, go to the pool, and watch television." He shrugged. "Whatever you want, except use the computer or the phone."

"Alone?"

"No."

"Are you going watch me?" I chuckled, but it came from nerves rather than humor. I didn't need to feed my growing attachment to Ryker. My situation reminded me of one of those 'don't feed the animals' signs. It only encouraged the animals to rely on humans for food. In my case, spending more time with Ryker would encourage my mushrooming addiction to him.

"No. We can't spend any more time together." Ryker opened the villa door, and I followed him inside. A twinge of disappointment twisted my gut, and my pathetic reaction only confirmed he was right. Spending more time together wasn't a good idea. Actually, it was a terrible idea.

The villa was just as I remembered it—a collage of warm jewel tones and creamy whites. An oversized, oil-rubbed bronze chandelier, dripping with hundreds of tiny diamond-shaped crystals, hung from the center of the vaulted ceiling. Light from the wall of windows reflected off the crystals, creating hundreds of miniature rainbows on the tile floor, walls, and furniture. I'd seen many impressive homes in my life, and this villa rivaled any of them.

Ryker turned right down the hallway and I followed him, treading four or five steps behind. "Where's the pool?" I asked. Logically, it should have been right out the living room doors, but I didn't see it when I escaped a couple days ago.

"On the side of the house." Ryker nudged the door open to a bedroom.

It resembled a smaller version of the one where Ryker left me a couple days ago. Same creamy bedding. Same honeyed wood. The throw blanket at the bottom of the bed was orange, cranberry, and dark chocolate instead of red and black. The ceilings weren't vaulted, but it looked nearly identical.

"Maybe you could bring me there next." I

wanted to swim some laps. Even though I had run through the jungle when I tried to escape, it didn't offer the same fix as structured exercise in a controlled environment. I ran and swam religiously at home. It kept me focused. It kept me in control.

"Javier will show you."

"Okay." I nodded. "That will work."

He stuffed his hands into his pockets and rocked back onto his heels. "Your clothes should be in the closet. Your toiletries should be in the bathroom. Your suitcase is under the bed. I had them put everything in here."

"What about my phone?"

"Except for your phone."

My shoulders slumped even as I knotted my hands into fists. I didn't expect a different answer. He may have granted me limited freedom, but it would be dumb to give me my phone, and Ryker wasn't dumb. Far from it. I squared my shoulders and cocked my chin to the side. "I wanted to call Vera."

"Your red-headed friend from the bar?" He rubbed the dark stubble on his chin with the top of his knuckles.

"Yes, that's Vera. I don't think my family will keep her in the loop, and I know she'll be worried about me." I shifted my weight from one foot to the other. "I know Vera, and she's blaming herself for what happened to me."

He sighed. "I'll think about it, but don't get your hopes up. It probably won't happen, and if it does, it won't be until a few hours before you're released."

"Am I going to be released soon?" I knew I

shouldn't prod him for answers. He had given me enough for one day, but I wanted to know.

"Everything hinges on the video conference tomorrow, but that's the plan."

"Will I see you later today?"

"No."

With that one word, he walked out of the room and my heart stumbled. I didn't know if I'd ever see him again, and I wasn't ready to say goodbye forever.

# Chapter Twenty-Three

The next morning, I had showered and put on my swimming suit and a sundress by the time someone knocked on my door.

I slept better last night than I had in a week. Total exhaustion—both mental and physical—probably had something to do with it, but I also attributed it to the comfort of the bed.

"Come in," I said as I slid my feet into my camel colored ballet flats. My feet hurt too much to wear any of my sandals.

Javier stood in my doorway with a food tray in his hand. He dressed in a version of the same outfit he always wore. White shirt. Khaki pants. Brown loafers. "*¿Desayuno?*" he asked. Then, he shook his head. "I'm sorry. Breakfast?"

"Thank you." I took the tray from him.

Yogurt, fresh fruit, and chia seeds. "How did you know?" I asked, my eyes searching his.

"Ryker requested it."

I nodded, my heart squeezing and my mind reeling. Ryker remembered my flippant comment about what I liked to eat in the morning. I didn't need any reminders of him. I needed to erase him from my system before he released me for good. "Of course."

"Ryker wants you to be ready for a video conference at ten in the morning," Javier said, backtracking a few steps.

"Wait," I said, putting the tray of food on my nightstand. My eyes flickered to the alarm clock. It was only eight-thirty. "Can you show me where the pool is? I want to swim this morning."

Javier rubbed his hands together. "Now?"

"Sure, or after breakfast. Either is fine."

Javier walked through the bedroom, stopping at the curtained window. He glanced over his shoulder. "Do you mind?"

"No," I answered, confused by his actions.

In one swift motion, he pulled back the floor to ceiling silk curtains. "The pool is right here." He swung the door open.

"Ryker said you liked to swim, so he selected this room for you."

"Oh." I didn't know what to say. Ryker knew I liked to swim. I guess he wasn't bluffing about keeping tabs on me before he abducted me. Conflicting emotions flashed through me, but I buried them for later introspection.

"You can use the pool anytime." He shifted on his feet. "Except at night."

"Why not at night?"

"Ryker swims at night," he answered simply, as though that's all he needed to say, and maybe it was.

"Okay. I'll keep that in mind."

"Anything else?" Javier asked, smile on his face.

"Why did you join the Vargas Cartel?" I couldn't stop myself from asking the question. Unlike Caesar who tried to kill me, Javier didn't belong here, or at least from what I'd seen of him.

He tipped up his chin and puffed out his chest as though he was offended by the suggestion. "I'm not part of the Vargas Cartel. I work for Ryker."

My mind stumbled. "Ryker? I thought he was part of the cartel."

"No. He's not." Javier answered without explanation.

"Does helping the cartel hide me and keep me captive bother you?"

"I'm helping Ryker. He saved my life. I'd do anything for him."

"How did he save your life?"

"Ten years ago, the Vargas Cartel broke into my home as a kid. Ryker was with them. I hid under the bed, but they found me. Ryker stepped between the gun and me and refused to let them kill my brother and me."

"Why did Ryker do it?"

"I don't know, but I'm grateful. He gave me a job and he has kept my family safe for ten years now. Anything else?"

"No."

"Okay, then be in the study by ten this morning for the video conference."

\*\*\*

202

Ten o'clock arrived faster than I had anticipated, and I ran through the house, my bare feet slapping against the tile floors, and my wet hair dripping onto the sleeves of my gray t-shirt.

"Hattie," Ignacio said, inclining his head the minute I breached the study door threshold.

"Yes?"

Ignacio pointed toward the chair behind the desk. "Please sit."

Hesitating, my foot froze mid-stride. Images of the first time I entered this room flashed through my mind, but I tamped down my fears and settled into the brown leather chair. I hoped this time ended better than the last time.

My eyes surveyed the room, taking note of every person. Javier. Caesar. The security guards with guns. No Ryker. "Where's Ryker?" I asked.

Ignacio tapped his fingers on the desk for a few excruciating ticks of the second hand. "Ryker is no longer involved in this mission on a daily basis."

Without any further explanation, he leaned toward the computer monitor and turned it on. After a few strokes of his fingers, I heard a ringing noise. Instead of hovering over the back of my chair like last time, Ignacio shifted to the side.

Two rings later, Evan, Senator Deveron, and my dad appeared on the screen. Tangible relief warmed my body, starting with my heart and spreading outward in the form of a warm, fuzzy glow. I missed my dad. I missed his dark hair, his even darker eyes, and the strong, firm set of his mouth.

"Dad," I said, my voice barely a whisper.

"Hattie," he said, drifting forward. "Are you

okay?

"I am now," I answered, not realizing how much I missed him and even my mom until right then.

"Are you hurt?" my dad pressed.

"Not really."

His eyes surveyed my face and my chest, clearly cataloging the scratches and bruises marring my skin from my failed attempts to escape. "What. Happened. Hattie?" Rage laced every word.

"Oh," I said, the pads of my fingers coasting down the side of my face. "It's my fault. I ran and—"

"Are they responsible for those marks?" my dad asked, interrupting my explanation.

"No," I said a little too animatedly. For some reason, I wanted to protect Ryker. Ryker did a lot of things to me, but he didn't hurt me physically. "It's from the trees, and I tripped a few times."

He nodded, but he looked unconvinced. "You'll be home soon, Hattie. Just hold on and be strong, okay?"

"I will." My voice quivered. "I love you, Daddy."

"We love you, too, Hattie," my dad answered.

Ignacio dropped his hand on my shoulder, and I flinched, despising the contact with him. "You can leave now."

I braced my hand on the armrests of the desk chair for a moment, not wanting to sever contact with my dad.

"Go ahead, Hattie," Senator Deveron interjected. "We have a few details to discuss in private, but Evan will meet you in Mexico when this is over."

"Okay," I answered, even though I didn't want Evan to meet me here. In an ideal world, I'd have a few days to unwind and deconstruct my thoughts before I faced him, but fate hadn't been kind lately. I didn't expect it to change course now.

# Chapter Twenty~Four

When I finished swimming my laps the following day, Ignacio was waiting at the edge of the pool. Just like every other time I'd seen him, he dressed in all black.

"I'd like you to take a drive with me," he said as I stepped out of the pool.

I draped my towel over my shoulders. "Do I have a choice?"

He chuckled, and for the first time I saw amusement in his dark eyes. "No, you don't."

I frowned. "I didn't think so. Can I dress first?"

He pointed to my navy and white striped cover up. "That will work. It's just a drive."

"Okay, then," I mumbled, pulling the cover up over my still damp hair and swimming suit.

"Follow me," he said without turning around as he started down the pathway to the front of the villa.

A black SUV sat in the driveway. Ignacio opened the front passenger door for me and he slipped into the driver's seat a minute later.

"No driver today?" I questioned as the car pulled

away from the house.

"Not today. I don't want any witnesses."

"What?" I said, my heart slamming against the walls of my chest.

He reached over and patted my leg before returning his hand to the steering wheel. "I don't plan to kill you."

"I'm not a target?" I questioned, recalling Ryker's conversation about cargo and targets.

Ignacio chuckled. "Nope, you're still cargo."

"Then why?" My mind scoured his face, searching for the answer in his eyes, but he was unreadable. "Wait. Am I leaving for good?" My words betrayed my excitement.

"Are you ready to go home?"

"Of course. Why would I want to stay?" The moment the words left my mouth, grief lanced through my chest. I wanted to go home, but I craved Ryker. I wanted—no, needed—to see him, touch him, talk to him, one more time before I disappeared from his life forever.

Ignacio smiled, but his eyes lacked warmth. "I think we both know why you want to stay—"

"I don't," I protested before he could finish his thought.

"If you say so, but you're not leaving us yet. We have to make a few more arrangements, but it shouldn't take longer than three or four more days. How's that sound?"

I sucked in my lower lip and ducked my head to hide my relief. "Perfect," I replied sarcastically, even though it was the truth. I had three or four more days to see Ryker. "So where are we going now?"

"For a drive to Highway 307."

"Isn't that the highway to the airport?"

"It is," Ignacio answered without glancing at me.

"Why are we going to the airport if I'm not going home?"

"We're not. We're going for a drive."

I slumped in the seat. "So we are," I mumbled.

"What do you know about the Vargas Cartel?"

"Other than that it smuggles drugs across the border? Not a lot."

His ebony eyes landed on mine. "Law enforcement agencies, on both sides of the border, describe drug cartels as snakes that grow another head as soon as the other is dismembered. It's interesting imagery, but this characteristic has allowed cartels to thrive despite the all-out war launched by the DEA and the Mexican government when former President Calderón took office in 2006."

Ignacio turned onto Highway 307.

"How did you get involved in the cartel?"

"When I graduated from high school, I became a police officer, but I quickly realized I could make more money working for drug smugglers. I worked my way up the chain of command, and here I am."

"So you've done it all?"

"I started at the bottom. I've donned a ski mask and dragged men away from crying wives and mothers. I've tied people up and cut them apart, piece by piece. I've hacked off heads. I've ordered countless assassinations." He spoke slowly, and his eyes were distant, almost unfocused. Otherwise, his face was void of emotion. "Living that life robbed me of my compassion, and I didn't want that for Rever. I wanted him to start at the top, and maybe that was my mistake. He didn't appreciate the gift I gave him."

Speechless, I shuddered, and bile burned the walls of my throat. If I stopped to think about it, Ignacio's confession wasn't surprising. I didn't believe anyone could make it to the top of the cartel without committing countless murders. I turned my head to the side, fixing my vision on the passing landscape, praying this car ride ended soon. "How can you live with yourself?" I whispered more to myself than Ignacio.

"I don't have a choice. Once you're in a cartel, the only way out is prison or death." He brought the car to a stop and turned off the ignition. "But I don't like either of those options, so I fight to maintain what's mine."

"You could disappear."

"Not anymore. I'm too high up the food chain, but that isn't the point of this drive." He tapped me on my leg, and my eyes met his. Any amusement I had seen in his eyes earlier this morning had disappeared. They were a black hole, sucking me into a void of emptiness. "The only way to bring your enemies down and save yourself is by annihilating their whole infrastructure: their police protection, their soldiers, their friends, their families, and their assets. You kill them before they can kill you." He pointed his finger directly in front of the car. "Dario's son."

Twenty yards in front of us, a boy, not older than

seventeen, was tied to a lamppost. His bloodied head lay sideways next to his feet, and a pig's head was placed on top of his corpse. A knife was buried in his chest, affixing a piece of white paper to his body. The sign said, "*VC captura y exucutes traidores.*"

"The Vargas Cartel captures and executes traitors," Ignacio whispered almost reverently. "The turf war between the Vargas and Alvarez Cartel has begun. Every cartel has a calling card of sorts. What do you think of ours?"

For a split second, I didn't do anything. My mouth gaped open, silently straining for air. I stared at the horror in front of me, my mind swirling with disbelief even as time slowed to a meager crawl. Then, the gravity of the vision in front of me struck me like a bolt of lightning, and my mind shattered into a million pieces. Air rushed into my lungs, and I screamed and screamed some more until my voice gave out, because I didn't know what else to do. When my shrieks of terror morphed into a soundless whisper, I buried my head in my hands, my entire body shaking.

At some point, Ignacio started driving again, but I refused to open my eyes. I refused to look at him. It was official: I was living in a nightmare.

# Chapter Twenty-Five

One sunset turned into four, and before I realized it, four days had elapsed since my drive with Ignacio. I had slipped into a routine, which did wonders for my obsessive need to schedule and organize my life down to the last detail. More importantly, it kept my mind off the murder scene Ignacio showed me, and I pretended as though it hadn't happened—at least until I fell asleep. Then, the nightmares overwhelmed my unconscious mind, and I rarely slept more than four for five hours.

Javier brought me a light breakfast every morning at eight. I swam laps until my muscles ached. Then, I read books from the comfort of a shaded lounge chair by the pool. I showered at three in the afternoon, and I ate dinner at five in my room.

Ignacio invited me to join him for dinner every night, but I declined. Even though I wondered if I'd see Ryker at dinner, my need to avoid Ignacio overshadowed my desire to see Ryker. I wasn't ready to see Ignacio. I didn't know if I'd ever be ready.

After dinner, the torture began—not physical but mental.

The first night, it started with a simple splashing noise in the pool around ten at night. Curious, I had peeked out my curtains, and I saw Ryker swimming laps in the pool. Every night since, I had left my drapes open while I sat in the comfort of my bed with the lights off, watching Ryker swim back and forth for nearly an hour.

He knew I watched him, but he never acknowledged me. He never let his eyes drift to my window. He never waved. He swam and then returned to his room. It was like I didn't exist, had never existed. Maybe it was better that way...for both of us.

"Can I come in," Ignacio pushed the door open to my room as I finished my last bite of breakfast.

"Sure." My hands shook as I placed my spoon on the tray, and I moved to stand up from the bed.

"You don't have to get up." He walked past me to the window overlooking the pool, pausing there with his back turned to me and his hands clasped behind his body. I was grateful he didn't sit next to me on the bed. I waited for him to say what he needed to say and leave. I hated being in the same room with him.

"You're leaving tomorrow. Before breakfast. It's all arranged," he muttered.

I clutched the folds of my skirt and nodded, unable to look at him even if it was only his back. "Okay." I forced myself to remain calm and keep my voice even. He scared me and tied my mouth in knots. When I looked at him, I saw a monster. A soulless, heartless monster.

He cast a glance over his shoulder, and a small smile tugged at the corners of his normally grim mouth. "We finished negotiations yesterday. I planned to tell you at dinner last night, but you declined as usual."

"Sorry," I lied, but I didn't know what else to say. I didn't want to be alone with him. Even sharing the same room and air filled me with a sickening rage.

"No, you're not." He spun around and leaned against the wall. "I get it. You think I'm a bad person because you don't think I feel any guilt over the things I've done, the people I've killed."

The statement hung in the air, weighing it down. I drew my knees up to my chest and rested my head on my knees. "Is there any other way to look at it?" I asked, my voice hardly a rasp.

Pushing away from the wall, he expelled a heavy breath and stuffed his hands into his pockets. "I improve the lives of the members of my cartel. I make sure they adhere to a code of ethics, which includes embracing family values. None of my members abuse drugs, and if they do, we clean them up and then they work for me to repay the favor of saving their lives. My members attend mass regularly. I give loans and gifts to local schools, businesses, farmers, and churches. We are so much more than a cartel smuggling drugs. We are a social organization. We bring order and meaning into the lives of the poor."

"Really?" Stunned by his admission, I didn't

know what to say. I never considered a cartel might do as much good and as it does bad. Not everything was black and white.

"I help people. The Vargas Cartel is a necessary evil, but you wouldn't understand. How could you? You've never lived in Mexico. You've never been poor and without resources."

"No, I haven't," I admitted.

"We don't kill women. We don't kill innocent people, only those who deserve to die."

"Nobody deserves to die." My gut lurched as I said the words. I killed a man. I did it in self-defense, but maybe I had lost the moral authority to judge Ignacio the minute I pulled the trigger.

"Your innocence is almost charming." A condescending smile spread across his face. "Have you talked to Ryker?"

I shook my head. "No, not since he showed me to this room, but I'm sure you already knew that."

A lopsided grin pulled at his mouth for a second. "The cameras."

"Yes, the cameras," I snapped, not even trying to moderate my voice.

"So you're planning to walk away without saying another word to him."

I swallowed over the sudden tightness in my throat. "That's what he wants."

His nearly black eyebrows arched. "Are you sure about that?

"Yes." My voice faltered, and I sounded unsure, confused even. "But even if it isn't, you made it clear that you'd ruin my life if I didn't stay away from him."

He nodded. "Ah, we're back to the video and the cameras." He strolled across the room, his hands in his pockets. "Maybe that's what is wrong with your generation."

"What?" I answered, not understanding why I bothered prolonging this conversation. How in the hell would he know if something was wrong with my generation? He was a sick and twisted murderer.

"You've been handed everything without working for it, so you're afraid to go after what you really want in life. You settle for mediocrity when you should go after your dreams. Mediocre spouses. Mediocre careers. Mediocre lives." He shook his head, disdain dripping from his voice. "How boring."

"And murdering your way to the top of a cartel was your dream?" I taunted, the smugness in Ignacio's voice grating on my already threadbare nerves.

"Being the best at whatever I did was my dream."

"And you're the best."

"I'd like to think so." The declaration sounded almost serene. He opened the door. "Have your things packed and be waiting by the front door at seven in the morning. Take care, Miss Covington, and good luck with your life." He paused with his hand on the doorknob. "With whatever you choose or don't choose."

What the hell did that mean? "And if I choose Ryker?"

"Then you choose Ryker."

I rubbed my hands together. "You won't do

215

anything to stop me."

"No. I got what I wanted."

"And what was that?"

"Your compliance until I could secure Rever's release. I've secured his release, so what you do or don't do isn't my concern."

# Chapter Twenty~Six

"Ignacio plans to release me tomorrow," I said when he reached the end of the pool. Drops of water glistened like stars on his tanned skin.

His muscles tensed, but he didn't acknowledge me. He dove back under the surface of the water, going back and forth at least six more times. Desperate for him to acknowledge me, to talk to me, I shrugged off my sundress, exposing my white bikini. I lowered myself into the pool, waiting by the edge for him to finish his laps.

"I wanted to say goodbye," I said when he surfaced again only inches from me.

"You need to go."

I ignored him. "You haven't said one thing to me in five days."

"That's by design." He sidestepped me, moving toward the steps exiting the pool.

"Stop." I wrapped my hands around his biceps, refusing to let him walk away from me again, refusing to let him do anything but look me in the eye and talk to me. "Why won't you talk to me?"

He kept his head turned, not meeting my gaze. "You can't even look at me."

The awkwardness between us was palpable, and I hated it. For some reason, I had deluded myself into believing he cared about me. I shouldn't have tried to talk to him. I should've stayed in my room and waited for my last hours in captivity to expire. I had read too much into the time we spent together, which was ridiculous on my part, given the circumstances of how we met.

I shifted nervously from one foot to the other waiting for him to say something…anything.

"Hattie," he said, his gray eyes finally locking on mine. "Why'd you come?"

"You're right, I should go. This was a dumb idea. I don't know what I was thinking. If you wanted to talk to me, you had many opportunities to do so. I'm forcing you—"

"Shut up, Hattie." He pressed a finger to my mouth holding it there. "I don't know what you're thinking."

"That I should've stayed in my room. That I don't belong here."

"Neither do I." He dropped his hands to my shoulders, and he had this lost look on his face. My heart twisted. "I've never felt comfortable here. I hated the summers I spent in this house. I hated my dad's life, and I hated Rever. We were close in age, but we were never friends…more like polite enemies with an unspoken agreement to tolerate each other."

His eyes looked translucent in the moonlight. I couldn't tear my gaze from his face, and he didn't look away either. My body soaked up the attention. Physical awareness zipped between us like a live wire, and a warm glow shimmered through my nerve endings. Instantly, I tamped it down, doing everything to stop it. I couldn't go *there* again…for so many glaringly obvious reasons, not the least of which was my dignity.

I took a small step back, but he moved forward, and before I knew it he had me pressed against the wall, his legs tangling with mine beneath the waist-deep water. His arms circled my waist, shackling me against his chest. My insides jolted the minute our bodies made contact, and with that small touch I was already aroused, my body wanting his. My breasts ached. Liquid desire pooled between my thighs, and my heart raced frantically inside my chest, echoing wildly in my ears.

I buried my face in the crook of his neck, unable to look at him for one more second. I had wanted him, craved him, for the last five days, and now that his arms were around me, I was scared. "I'm going to leave," I murmured against the side of his neck. "I just wanted to say goodbye, and now I did." I took a deep breath, drawing his now familiar scent into my lungs for the last time. Then, I wedged my hands between our slick bodies, pushing him away from me forever.

Binding my wrists with one hand, he lifted my chin, forcing me to look at him. Really look at him. What I saw robbed me of thought and buckled my knees. It was too much. I squeezed my eyes closed. "No. You should stay." He brushed a kiss across my lips, my forehead and my eyelids. With four sultry caresses, he tore down all my walls, crumbling any lingering resistance. "Don't you want me?" He nuzzled my ear and tremors danced down my spine, setting me ablaze. "Isn't that why you're here?"

*Want him?* I had never wanted anyone as much as I wanted him, and not just in the physical sense. How could he think otherwise? Panic warred with desire at that realization, and I froze. I didn't know what to do. How did I move forward?

Then he kissed me—fully, deeply, desperately. I was cast adrift, senseless to anything around me but the push and pull of his mouth and the delicious swirl of his tongue as it chased mine in a circle of lust. If I didn't know everything between us ended tonight, I would've have wept from the beauty of the moment.

I slipped my legs around his waist, locking my ankles behind his back, whimpering as my core collided with the hardness of his erection. His hands cupped my breasts over the small triangles of my swimming suit. I arched, inviting him to do more.

Not waiting a second, he unknotted the ties holding the back of my top together and slipped it over my head. He tossed it on the side of the pool and then his hands were back on my breasts, roughly toying with my nipples until I was breathless and aching with the pain of emptiness.

"Ryker," I moaned, recklessly grinding my pelvis against his, against the thickness of his erection beneath his swim trunks.

He pulled the tie on one side of my bikini bottom and then the other, and they floated away from my body. His finger slipped inside of me, moving with wicked intent, in and out and back again. We were on a rollercoaster of desire and everything was moving too fast for my mind to process it.

"I missed this. I missed you," he whispered, nipping the delicate edge of my earlobe. His confession spiraled through me, and my heart skipped a beat, even though I knew I should ignore his words. Pretend I didn't hear them. Pray I unheard them. *It's only tonight*, I reminded myself. Wanting more, claiming this meant anything, was insane. It would destroy me. Destroy my life. Destroy me for anyone else.

I unlocked my ankles and shoved his swim trunks down his legs, not wanting to wait another second before he slid inside of me. I didn't want him to stop...to pull back. He'd done it before and I couldn't bear it if he stopped. I needed it. I needed him. I needed closure to whatever we had over the last three weeks, and this was the way I intended to get it.

He anchored my legs around his waist again, but this time I felt every inch of him, skin on skin, solid and pulsing with unfulfilled desire. I lifted my arms, wrapping them around his neck, pulling him closer, begging him with my body to take what we both needed...what we both wanted.

Then, he drove inside of me, stilling for a second, not moving. We both blew out a long, exaggerated breath of relief, our foreheads touching, our eyes connecting, our hearts beating together in perfect synchronicity. I didn't know what it meant. I didn't want to know. I was afraid the knowledge would kill me.

"Ryker," I murmured, sounding more than a little lost.

He nodded. "I know."

He pulled out, pushed in again, and then slid out once more. I tightened my legs, pulling him closer, hating the split second where I lost that primal connection to him. He slid his hand around my hips, cupping my backside, and then he moved fast and hard. My back pounded against the walls of the pool, scraping my skin, but I hardly noticed.

Distantly, I heard the slapping of the water as it lapped over the tiled ledge of the pool, and the small noises of birds and insects in the jungle surrounding us. But most of all, I heard the sounds of us.

Skin slapped against skin.

Exhalations mingled into one solid stream of desire.

Moans chased moans.

I curled into him, trusting him to keep me afloat, not just physically, but mentally too.

Hot, glowing fire blazed through my body coalescing in my core. I was close. So close. My nails raked his back. An answering shudder wracked through his body. Our pleasure climbed to completion in unison, coiling tighter and tighter with each thrust and roll of his hips.

Then, I climaxed, fast and hard. I screamed, not caring about anything. Not the cameras. Not Ignacio's security team. Not tomorrow. Not my freedom. Nothing except the feel of Ryker inside of me.

His mouth captured mine, drinking the tortured

sounds of my pleasure as spasm after spasm rocked through me, each one milking him to his completion. And then he came, following me into oblivion.

I swallowed his strained growl as his body stiffened against mine, and then he bucked with the force of his orgasm, slamming me into the wall one final time.

Neither of us moved for a prolonged second, basking in the warm glow of a shared release. Then, his body sagged against mine, his chin resting on my head, and his weight nearly pulled us under the water. I reached back, bracing my arms on the ledge of the pool.

"Sorry," he chuckled, taking a step back.

A satisfied smile on my face, I leaned against the wall and tipped my head to the sky. The sky was a maze of brilliant, shimmering diamonds on black velvet.

"It's beautiful at night here," I whispered without meeting his eyes.

"You're beautiful at night," he answered immediately.

Happiness, exhilaration, and exhaustion collided inside of me. I didn't know if I wanted to swim a hundred laps or crawl back to my room and sleep.

He scooped me up in his arms, carrying me out of the pool.

"Where are we going?" My arms circled his neck, and I buried my face against his damp chest.

"To your room."

"The cameras," I whispered. Ignacio said he didn't care what happened between Ryker and me, but I still didn't want him to have any evidence to use against me at some date in the future.

"I turned them off." He pushed the door to my room open.

"When?"

"Earlier tonight. Before I got into the pool." His wet feet slapped against the terra cotta tiles.

"Why?"

"Because if you didn't come to me, I planned to go to you."

I tipped my face up so I could see him. "But you told me to go away and that we shouldn't do this anymore. You didn't want me."

A grin lit the shadowed planes of his sharp-angled face. "I wanted you. I've always wanted you, but I needed to give you the chance to say no if that's what you wanted."

He let my feet drop to the floor, next to the bed. He stripped back the covers. "Get in."

"Wait," I said as I sat down. "Our swimming suits."

"I'll get them before morning."

"Are you leaving?"

"No." His eyes flashed to the clock, glowing with red numbers on the nightstand. "We still have five hours and forty-five minutes until you leave, and I intend to put every minute we have left to good use."

My eyes widened, and he chuckled. "Make room for me."

I scooted back, my eyes never leaving his.

Almost instantly, his body covered mine, his lips drinking me in, demanding all of me. And we were right back where we started, touching each other, devouring each other, taking more than either of us had the right to give.

Each frenzied kiss and wild touch tumbled into the next. His mouth consumed me. His teeth marked me, but I didn't complain. I wanted him to claim me even if it was only for a night…less than a night.

Then, he slid inside of me for the second time that night, claiming me like I'd never been claimed before. Like I'd never be claimed again. Every thrust stole more of me than the previous one. Every wave of pleasure swallowed my regrets and any lingering 'what ifs,' because Ryker and I could never be anything except what we were in this fragment of time.

Then, like a perfectly orchestrated dance, we climaxed in unison, the agony and beauty of the moment making me delirious—deliriously happy and deliriously sad.

# Chapter Twenty-Seven

"Hattie."

I rolled onto my side, pulling the sheets over my head.

"Hattie," the voice said again. "You need to wake up. You're leaving in twenty minutes."

My eyes snapped open and then I shut them immediately, blocking the blinding sun streaming through the windows.

"Close the fucking curtains," I grumbled.

"No. We overslept."

"Ryker?" I said, opening my eyes again, squinting to bring him into focus.

Ryker was fully dressed in his usual black pants and black shirt. His hair was wet and his face was clean-shaven.

"I moved your suitcase to the car. Everything is ready for you to leave."

"Crap," I said, sitting up, the sheet falling to my waist, making me uncomfortably aware of the fact that I was still naked while he had dressed and showered.

"You don't have time to shower."

He handed me a stack of clothes. I stared at them, unseeing for a few moments.

"Let me help you."

"No," I answered reflexively. I needed to put some distance between us.

He ignored me. Instead, he snagged the clothes out of my hands and within seconds he started dressing me. First, he slid on my panties, then my bra and finally, my dress. The protectiveness and intimacy in his gesture made the corners of my eyes burn with tears I could never shed.

"You look beautiful." He trailed a finger down my neck and along my collarbone. Our eyes locked, exchanging words and thoughts better left unspoken. Misery boomeranged through my body. Whatever we had was over, and I'd never see him again.

"You should put some makeup on your neck."

I shrugged because I didn't care about my neck.

"And comb your hair. It looks like you spent the night rolling around in bed." He smirked as he handed me the comb from the nightstand. I ran it through my hair before tossing it on the bed.

He glanced over his shoulder.

"Wait." I snagged his arm. "Are you leaving? Is this it?"

He smiled, but his eyes looked dull and flat. "Not yet. First, I'm going to kiss you. Then, I'm going to walk you to the car, say goodbye, and you're going to drive away."

"Okay." My body swayed with the impending loss.

He swept a strand of hair behind my ear. "You're going to meet Evan where highway 307 intersects with the road leaving the villa. Then, you're going to forget about me, about what happened between us, and you're going to give Evan his second chance."

"No, I can't." I shook my head from side to side, nausea rising in my stomach.

He pressed to fingers to my lips. "You can, and you will."

"But…" I protested.

He cradled my face with the palms of his hands. "But nothing, Hattie. What we had or didn't have is over. Wanting or wishing for something else won't change the future."

Tears leaked from my eyes, and I didn't bother wiping them away. I simply stood there waiting for the kiss he promised. I didn't have another option. What he said was the cold truth.

His lips brushed across mine for the hundredth time in the last seven hours, but unlike last night, this kissed wasn't frenzied or an invitation for more. It was goodbye. I followed his lead, tasting him, memorizing him, and absorbing the beauty of the end of us.

And then he released me, and it was over. Forever.

# Chapter Twenty-Eight

I switched the gearshift into drive. I was free. I should have said a Hallelujah or two, but my freedom felt flat, lonely, and oppressive. I inhaled deeply through my nose to push back the rush of despair flooding my veins.

Yes, Evan and my old life would be waiting for me where the road met the highway, just like Ryker said. I should've been happy, and I was. Within twenty-four hours, I'd be back in my bed at either my parents' house or my apartment with Evan. It was my choice.

Except, part of me didn't want that life anymore. I'd driven a hundred yards down the road, and I already missed Ryker. I craved him with every inhalation and exhalation. Somehow over the past few weeks, he infected my blood. He infiltrated my mind and ruined me for anyone else. With every touch and brush of his lips, he shattered the illusions of my former life and everything I believed about myself.

I wanted him in my life, which was fucking

stupid considering how he turned my life upside down and inside out. He abducted me, he used me to secure his brother's release, but my heart refused to believe he didn't care about me as much as I cared about him. His actions, his touch, and his eyes all said he felt something for me, but I didn't know what to believe anymore. I didn't trust him; but more importantly, I didn't trust myself.

He took everything I offered him and more last night, and now I wanted it again. I wanted more. His uniquely Ryker scent still coated my body, burning my senses and taunting me with his absence. The ghost-like memory of his embrace as he held me last night lingered in the air, teasing me. The weight of his body against mine as he moved inside me was like an invisible blanket, covering every inch of my skin, branding me for life.

And that kiss…I shouldn't have let that happen. I should've refused him and walked away, but that was the problem. I could never deny Ryker anything.

I slammed my hand against the steering wheel with a muttered curse. What the fuck was I thinking? I'd never see him again. I refused to believe otherwise, and wanting anything from him, even for a split second, was dangerous. "Move on, dammit. Move the fuck on!" I screamed in the empty car.

I knew Ryker was trouble from the first minute my eyes met his in that bar. If my ego hadn't been bruised and battered by Evan's betrayal, I would have walked away without a second glance and never looked back. Ryker said he would have found me anyway, but maybe things would have been different. Maybe I could've eluded him. Maybe I would've found someone else at the bar. Who the heck knows?

I shook my head and white-knuckled the steering wheel. I needed to put distance between Ryker and me. Distance would make everything better. This thing with Ryker, whatever it was or wasn't, had ended. My sanity depended on my ability to scrub every last memory of him from my mind, my body, and my soul. What happened between us was my secret. I couldn't share it…ever. Nobody would understand. When I felt stronger, I could come to terms with my behavior and make sense of it, but I had a feeling it would be a long, hard road before I succeeded.

As the trees cleared, I saw the highway about two hundred feet in the distance.

Highway 307.

The highway to freedom.

The highway to Evan.

The highway to my family.

The highway to my old life.

The highway away from Ryker…forever.

Forever was a long time.

I swallowed my heated sobs and wiped the evidence of my tear-stained face with the back of my hand. It was over, and just as the thought floated through my mind, I saw Evan leaning against a black sedan on the shoulder of the road, his sandy brown hair blowing in the wind, and his hands shoved deep into the front pockets of his perfectly starched khaki pants. Even from a distance, I noticed the wide smile on his face. That charming smile used to make my stomach flip, now it made it twist. He cheated, but what I did was infinitely worse. I betrayed him with my mind, body, and soul. Going back to my old life, pretending as though nothing happened, didn't seem possible. But what options did I have?

I bit down hard on my lip until I tasted blood. "You can do this," I whispered to myself, even as my mind begged me to thrust the gearshift into reverse and run back to Ryker. We were over. I needed to accept it and move forward, just like Ryker said.

I'd face Evan and my family alone. I'd spent the next god knows how long weaving elaborate lies about my time as a prisoner because Ryker's name would never fall from my mouth ever again. He may own my body and a twisted part of my heart, but he wouldn't own my words. "Let the games begin," I said as I rolled down the window. The salty sea air washed over my skin and calmed my tattered nerves until the numbness swallowed me just as I had hoped.

# Chapter Twenty~Nine

*Ryker*

I raked my hands through my hair as I watched the back of Hattie's car until it disappeared into the twisted vines and shrubs of the jungle. Only then did I pull my cell phone from my front pocket. "Senator Deveron, Miss Covington has been released."

"Hold on, let me put my phone on speaker. My son will want to hear this too."

I gritted my teeth, barely holding back the anger I wanted to unleash on both of them. "Fine," I said through clenched teeth.

"Okay, go ahead," Senator Deveron said.

"You can retrieve Miss Covington where the road leading from the compound intersects with Highway 307 in twenty minutes. She'll be driving a light blue sedan," I said.

"Perfect. Rever's plane landed an hour ago. He should contact you soon."

"He already did," I offered. I wouldn't have let Hattie drive away if I didn't have confirmation of his release.

"Mr. Vargas, this is Evan Deveron."

"Yes?" I responded with thinly veiled disgust dripping from my voice. I hated this fucking asshole from the moment an acquaintance introduced me to him, and that was before I met Hattie.

"I trust that Hattie will be untouched and in good condition." Evan wanted to sound calm and business-like, but his voice wavered. He'd never be half the politician his father was, which was a good thing. He actually had a conscience living somewhere inside of him. Unfortunately for him, a conscience was a fatal flaw in D.C.

"Are you questioning how I do my job? You hired me to make you look like a fucking hero. Don't question my methods, or I'll drag her ass back here and you'll never get your second chance," I barked through the phone, refusing to answer Evan's question. After last night, there was no way anyone could call Hattie untouched. In fact, I made a point to touch every inch of her so I'd be so far under her skin, it'd be my face she'd see anytime Evan or any other stuffy asshole touched her.

"No," Senator Deveron said. "We understood the terms. As long as we find Hattie alive at the arranged meeting point, we'll be thrilled with your services. Evan will have his second chance, and Rever won't have the opportunity to reveal any undesirable information."

*Asshole.* He didn't give a shit about Hattie. He needed the merger of the Deveron and Covington families so he had the U.S. Attorney General in his pocket—in case the media or anyone else stumbled on his less-than-legitimate connections to the dirty money of the Mexican underworld. It funded his campaigns. It bought his casino. It bought his hookers. "Send your fucking people in here to clean up this place. I don't want any evidence connecting me to this shit."

"They're already on their way. It was a pleasure doing business with you again. One of these days, we'll have to meet in person and discuss how I can get you to work for me full time. I'm going to run for President soon."

"I never do business with people I haven't met." It wasn't a lie. I never took a job without weaving myself into the person's world beforehand. They may not know my real name or line of work, but I made sure I knew everything about them.

"We've met?" Senator Deveron's voice wavered, exhibiting an uncharacteristic flicker of insecurity.

I chuckled, finding amusement in exposing his fear. "Of course. I know everything about you, including your weekly call to that escort service in Fairfax. Your Christian constituents back home wouldn't look favorably on that information."

His anger vibrated through the phone, but he didn't scare me. Nobody did. Unlike my father, I bartered in information. Money didn't rule the world. Information did, and I had it in spades. I owned everyone.

"Son," Ignacio Vargas said, putting his hand on my shoulder as I disconnected my burner phone and removed the battery. "Did everything work out?"

"Just as we discussed." I slipped the phone into my pocket.

"And Senator Deveron's connections to the Vargas Cartel won't be exposed?"

"Not today." I crossed my arms over my chest. My life as a fixer wore on me, especially when my family sucked me back into the fold to deal with their shit. When I started in my line of work, I loved being the force behind the scenes, manipulating the world to right it again. Now I realized my naivety. There weren't any good or bad guys. They were on the same fucking team, working for the same fucking goal. The struggle between the righteous and the evil was world-class theater to manipulate the masses into tiny pockets of fear and hatred. After all, it's easier to control people divided than people united.

I needed to make some drastic changes in my life. I knew that. I knew it for the last twelve months. I never intended to stay in my current line of work indefinitely, anyway. I always had other plans…other goals, and now it was time to move forward. My untimely feelings for Hattie complicated things, but I had a plan, and I needed to see it through.

"Are you going to stay for a few more days?" Ignacio asked, interrupting my wandering thoughts.

"I'm afraid not," I said, my voice completely void of emotion.

"I could use your help," Ignacio replied. "Things are going to be crazy now that the Alvarez Cartel has claimed some of my territory."

Ten years had elapsed since the last time Ignacio asked me to help him with the Cartel. Rever didn't have it in him to fill the role my dad had groomed him for since he took his first gulp of air. Ignacio realized that now, but it was too late. Leaders were born, not made—and Rever wasn't a leader. Not even close. He was weak. Ignacio knew it, I knew it, and so did every cartel in Mexico. He'd never be the leader Ignacio craved.

"I can't. I have other responsibilities. My next job starts in a few days."

Ignacio nodded staring into the darkness. "It should have been you, not Rever."

"Rever's your legitimate son." I could have said more, but no other words were necessary. We both knew the score, but his words meant more to me than I'd ever admit. A black sedan pulled up in front of the Villa. "This is my ride."

"Take care of yourself." Ignacio handed me my black lambskin briefcase. Except my computer, Senator Deveron's cleaners would destroy all of my personal items with the rest of the evidence. Like every other job, I disappeared without a trace when it ended—a ghost with two identities, floating between two countries and two lives.

"Thanks." I slipped into the back seat of the car.

"Ryker?" my dad said, his hand braced on the top of the door.

"Yes?"

"Are you going after her?"

"Miss Covington?" We both knew he meant Hattie.

My dad chuckled. "Yes, her."

"Why would I go after her? The job is over. Everyone got what they wanted."

"Except you."

"What do you mean?"

"You don't think I noticed someone turned off the cameras in her room last night, or that someone deleted the video feed of the pool?" He shook his head in disbelief, a low, harsh laugh escaping his mouth.

"I don't know what—"

"I'm not going to hurt her." His voice was uncharacteristically soft. "She's important to you, and that makes her important to me."

Stunned, I didn't respond immediately, but then I saw the sincerity in his face, and I believed him. "I haven't decided. I don't know if she's worth the hassle. My life is complicated." My stomach revolted, hating my answer, and I clenched my jaw, biting back the emotion. She was worth that and more, but the layers upon layers of lies and an impenetrable wall of complications stood between her and me.

"So that's what you're telling yourself." Ignacio shook his head, his eyes distant. "I didn't go after your mother. I regretted it." He combed his hands through his salt and pepper hair. My dad looked old and tired, no longer the larger than life man I remembered from my youth. I had been so caught up in my attraction to Hattie, I barely noticed. "I still do, every day. She was the love of my life. Time and distance can't alter true love."

Ignacio had closed the door before I formed a response, as though he hadn't turned my world upside down. My mom never found someone to love after she walked away from my dad. She lived in the past rather than the present, constantly reliving memories rather than creating new ones. All the while, Ignacio had a family, abundant wealth, and an army of servants.

She never complained, though. In fact, she always said she'd rather live alone than be a mistress or spend her life with someone she didn't love. I shook my head to clear the emotional turmoil bubbling under the surface.

"Good evening, Mr. Vargas."

"Thanks for changing your plans, Javier. I hate dragging you away from your wife and kids so early in the morning, but I have a flight to catch."

"No problem, sir. I understand."

I opened my laptop and scanned through my email. *Fuck.* I forgot about my afternoon meeting with Rever. "When you drop me off at the airport, call my brother and tell him my plans have changed. Ignacio wanted me to debrief him today, but I need to be in D.C. by this evening. He'll have to do it himself."

"Of course."

# Acknowledgments

Thank you for purchasing my book. I can't even begin to put to words what it means to me to be able pursue my love of writing. Thanks to Limitless Publishing for continuing to support me and to Rachel Whitwam for editing this book and helping me with ending. Thanks to my husband for giving me feedback. Finally, thanks to my long time friend Fatima Simon for helping me with the Spanish dialogue. All errors are my own.

# About the Author

After spending years practicing law and a million other things, Lisa decided to pursue her dream of becoming a writer and she must confess that inventing characters is so much more fun than writing contracts and legal briefs. A native of Colorado, she lives with her husband and three children in Denver.

**Facebook:**
https://www.facebook.com/lcardiff11

**Twitter:**
https://twitter.com/lcardiff_author

**Website:**
http://lisacardiff.com/

**Goodreads:**
https://www.goodreads.com/author/show/7692079.
Lisa_Cardiff